Mukat's Heart:
A Sunny Morgan Mystery

Mukat's Heart:
A Sunny Morgan Mystery

Cynthia Smead

Published by Debra Smith
2015

First Printing: 2015

ISBN 978-0-692-53816-6

Publisher
Debra Smith
PO Box 27466
Scottsdale, AZ 85255

Ordering Information:

Special discounts are available on quantity purchases by corporations, associations, educators, and others. For details, contact the publisher at the above address.

U.S. trade bookstores and wholesalers: Please contact the publisher Debra Smith at the above address.

Dedication

This book is dedicated to my mother Cynthia Louise Smead with all the love in my heart and soul!

Love Your Daughter,
Debi Smith

Acknowledgements

Publishing this book is the realization of my mother, Cynthia Smead's dream. I would like to thank the people that have made this happen in her memory.

First of all, thank you Mom! Without you, there would be no book!

Over the years there were many people that inspired and guided my Mom in her fledgling writing career. I know that she often spoke of my Grandfather, Paul while she was writing the book and his experiences with the Riverside County Mounted Posse. She was able to incorporate into her stories those feelings he would share of exhilaration when a small child was found alive and well in the unforgiving desert, as well as the devastation and guilt when they couldn't be saved. She also spoke of her friend Molly who would push her to keep writing, even when it was hard. Molly was her coach, editor, and confidant.

I know that I am missing others that helped this amazing woman write her story and I am so thankful that you were part of her life, whether you provided insight, inspiration or were just there for her when she needed someone to bounce ideas around.

Finally, I'd like to thank a couple of people that helped me realize my mother's dream in publishing *Mukat's Heart*. Randa took on the role of editor, photographer and supporter. She inspired me to share my Mom's gift with others and I couldn't have done this without her! I'd also like to thank my daughter, Nika for her realistic portrayal of our young victim on the cover. We had great fun dressing her up and posing her as the sun began to set in the desert.

Preface

This preface is hard for me to write because I wish with all my heart that the author, my mother Cindy, was here to do it herself. After all, a preface is typically written by the author. When my mom died recently without publishing her book, it became a mission of love for me to see her dream realized. Years ago when my mom began writing this story, I was fortunate enough to be able to spend many hours with her talking about the plot, devising twists and turns, and sharing my experiences with Search and Rescue to bring some 'real life' to Sunny's story.

I think my Mom really related to Sunny. She had grown up in the Coachella Valley and had often ridden her horse over the same trails that Sunny travelled. She was raised with a heartfelt respect for the desert and the Native American Indians that lived there. Our family had a close relationship with a local Cahuilla Indian Medicine woman who had taught us how to bring the rain and whistle the wind. We also have a family of avid Search and Rescue volunteers, so it was no wonder that Sunny followed that path as well. This love of the desert, the Native American community and customs and a dedication to helping those in need were the very core of my Mom's soul. I'm so excited that she was able to bring all of these to life in Sunny's story. I hope you enjoy it as much as I do!

Introduction

Although stories of the Cahuilla Indian mythologies may vary, in Cahuilla culture legend speaks of the Creation Story; a tale of the creation of people believed to involve two brothers, Mukat (pronounced mook-ot) and his twin, Tamaioit (pronounced tam-my-oh-wit) who created the Earth and all who inhabit the land. Tamaioit, who was believed to be very competitive, worked so quickly to create his people that they were crudely made; sloppy. The brothers argued over the quality of their workmanship, and whose people were more beautifully made. Angry and embarrassed, Tamaioit took the people he had created and left. Mukat's people came alive; however, and began to speak many languages, one being the beautiful Cahuilla language. This became the chosen language for Mukat's people.

Prologue

July 7, 1999

A hammer rose high against the moon and fell, blood dripping from the rounded steel. Again and again it rose and fell long after the girl was dead. A knife flashed in the soft light and carved its art into her flesh. Gently, the man wrapped the bloodied clothes and body in a thin white sheet. He raised his hands toward the light and then, with tears welling in his eyes, he took the girl's hand, dipped it in her blood, and placed its imprint carefully on the pitiful shroud. With reverence, he lifted her onto the bed of the truck. Once again behind the wheel, he jammed the key into the ignition and twisted it. The engine sputtered and died but on the third attempt rumbled to life. His hands shook slightly in the yellow glare of the dashboard lights as he drove the truck slowly down the gravel road until he found a quiet, dark place to stop. He carried the small bundle across a sandy wash, laid it tenderly under a thick salt cedar shrub and covered it with gravel. A coyote, fat from a season of good hunting, laughed a harsh barking call. The man quickly surveyed the moonlit landscape, expecting to catch a glimpse of the trickster. *Damn Indian legends!* The hair on the man's neck prickled. *Not this time, coyote! Her heart is mine.*

Clenching and unclenching his soft hands, he trod heavily back to the truck. Light was beginning to flood the eastern sky but had yet to touch the lifeless child. She would not feel the sun when it finally spread its fingers through the leaves. She would never feel anything again.

By the pre-dawn light, he climbed into the cab of the truck, started the engine again and pulled away rapidly, spraying gravel behind him. He drove down I-10 toward Palm Springs reveling in how effortless it was this time. The girl had been waiting for him near the bus stop. She wiggled her thumb at him and thrust out her slender hip. She couldn't have been more than eleven or twelve, but pretended to be older. She said she'd taken her half-sister to a little kid's party but she was still wearing the cone-shaped hat. He snickered as he relived the last few days. The girl's chatter had amused him but suddenly she stopped talking when he exited the freeway. He saw the beginnings of fear on her face.

"Don't worry. Have to pick up some stuff at the house. Won't take long."

For the next twenty minutes the girl stared out the passenger window without saying anything. At last she grew uneasy with the silence. "I hate the desert!"

"I know what you mean. Not much for a kid to do."

"You got that right." She smiled at him for the first time since they left the freeway.

"You hungry?" he ventured.

She glanced warily at him. "Um, yeah."

He concealed his excitement behind a placid smile. "I'll fix us something to eat. Nothing fancy. Maybe some hot dogs or something?"

She nodded

He pulled the truck into the driveway. "Come in if you want."

She hesitated. "I'll wait in the truck."

He shrugged his shoulders, "Suit yourself, but once we're on the freeway I'm not going to stop. Use the bathroom now while I'm fixing lunch or wait until we get to L.A."

He saw the indecision on her face and smiled when she opened the door of the truck and hesitantly followed him inside.

The girls' eyes widened. "God, whadja do? Rob an Indian graveyard?" She gazed around the room at glass-covered cabinets containing arrowheads, pieces of bone, pots, and baskets.

The man replied warily, "I paid good money for them!"

"I thought you couldn't do that anymore."

He swaggered with pride. "I have connections. Beautiful aren't they?"

"Yeah, you heard about peyote?"

"I heard about it." He grinned. "Bathroom's right over there." He pointed to a doorway covered by a Navajo rug. "Clean towels in the cabinet. I'll get the dogs on. Wanna soda?"

"Yeah. Thanks."

"Pepsi?"

"Okay."

She came out of the bathroom smoothing her hair with wet hands and perched lightly on the barstool as if ready to take flight if he came too close.

He watched impatiently as she slathered the hot dog with mustard and bit hungrily into it. She washed it down with the Pepsi he'd poured over a couple of ice cubes into a red plastic cup. She slammed the cup on the counter. "Yuck! This is gross!"

"All I had was diet. Sorry."

"You got some chips or somethin'?"

He went to the cupboard, grabbed an open bag of potato chips and gave it to her. She took a handful of stale chips and stuffed them in her mouth. He cautiously moved around the counter and eased himself closer to her. He sneered with disdain as he watched her devour the chips and lick the last salty crumbs from her fingers. "Greedy child!"

Her fear was palpable now, but before she could pull away his hands were on her. He stroked her long, brown hair gently at first, and then yanked her head back.

She screamed and tried to scratch his face with her ragged, bitten nails, but the man grabbed her thin wrist and violently twisted her arm behind her back.

"Shut up! Shut up or I'll hurt you bad."

She struggled with all her young strength until the drug he'd put in the soda began to slow her frantic efforts. She realized that she couldn't get away from him. "Please don't hurt me. I'll do anything. Don't hurt me!"

Her groveling filled him with desire. The girl slumped unconscious into his arms. The man looked lovingly at her. "Only I can save you now."

A few nights later he carried her lifeless body out to his truck. The man snickered, "The child is sanctified." He took the Palm Springs off ramp; the girl's screams still echoed in his head, her fear lingered as a sweet taste on his tongue. He felt his flaccid member pulsing with blood again, pushing up above his slacks. Shivers of pleasure surged through him. He didn't expect anyone to be home and confidently drove up to the garage. The porch light suddenly glared into his eyes. His pleasure collapsed. Angrily he slammed the door of the truck and stomped inside.

Chapter 1

June 1, 1999
Twin Palms Sheriff's Station

My name is Sunny Morgan. I'm a volunteer deputy for the Desert Sheriff's Posse Mounted Search and Rescue Unit. I ride a horse and I carry a gun. I'd been a member for two years when I made an ominous decision that put my life and the lives of those I love on the line. I should have known better, but sometimes I disregard the importance of being a team player. My story begins at a Tuesday night mandatory meeting.

Two members of the posse were standing outside the conference room of the new Sheriff station when Brad Johnson. The posse president, called the meeting to order.

"Come on people, let's get this meeting underway." He turned to me. "Sunny, tell Rick and Smitty to get in here. We've got a long agenda."

"You bet!" A woman with a mission, I marched out into the brightly lit hallway. "What's keeping you guys?"

"Sunny?" Smitty glanced at Rick who nodded his head affirmatively. Sometimes there's an attitude of superiority the *real* deputies show the volunteers that irritates me. It wasn't a good beginning for our meeting tonight.

"Two girls have disappeared in the last couple of months. You were on the search for the Wilson girl, weren't you?"

"Uh huh, but we didn't find her. A hiker found her body. You know something I don't?"

"Officially we haven't made a statement to the public, but we may have a serial killer on the loose. The MO was the same in both disappearances."

Smitty breathed deeply, shaking off the seriousness of the conversation. "Let's go Rick. There's posse work to do. I'll fill you in later." He forced his mouth into a lopsided grin, "Sunny, take us to our leader."

When I joined the Desert Posse, I expected I'd get a call, jump on my horse, and ride out to find people who were lost. It didn't take me long to discover there's a lot more to being a volunteer posse member: mandatory meetings once a month, law enforcement classes, and weekly training session in tracking and survival skills. The posse gets called out to provide security at golf tournaments and special events, patrol the local county fairgrounds, and ride night shifts at the mall during holidays. To protect the civilians, even our horses must pass rigorous testing before they can participate in any posse event.

I do my community service without complaints and try not to get sucked into politics and power struggles. My passion is search and rescue. If you're ever lost in the desert, I've been trained to find you.

After roll call the committee chairpersons reported on old business. My mind was clamoring with the possibility that the recent abductions were the work of a serial killer. It wasn't until Brad called on Jan Worthman, the deputy who's in charge of special events, that I started paying attention to what was on the agenda.

"Next month's training will be on Saturday, July tenth in Whitewater Canyon. Patty Kimball has offered us her ranch as a command post and camping area. We'll meet there at 7:00 a.m. and divide up into two or three teams depending on how many of you sign up.

Rick stood up. "Are we all going to work on the same scenario?"

Brad shook his head. "No. Each team will be given a separate training scenario. After you've successfully completed the exercise, and of course you will ... right? We'll meet back at Patty's place for a barbecue bash. Those of you who spend the night will be treated to a traditional posse breakfast on Sunday morning.

"Bring your significant others. The more the merrier. They can stay in camp during the morning training session. Nothing like mixing a little business with a lot of pleasure. Any questions?"

Dewayne Smith, also known as Smitty, stood up. He had a very serious expression on his lean, coffee-brown face, but there was a twinkle in his jet-black eyes. "And who's in charge of the food?"

Brad stroked his graying mustache and with an equally serious expression proclaimed, "From the treasurer's report I concluded that the posse can afford to buy the meat for the barbecue. The sheriff's mobile kitchen will be there for Sunday breakfast but the Saturday night barbecue's going to be potluck. Let Patty know what you're bringing." Brad couldn't keep a straight face any longer. "Smitty, now don't you worry. We aren't about to let you starve." That brought laughter from the rest of the group. "Now, one more item that isn't on the agenda. I have a letter here from the Chief congratulating us on the successful recovery of Lucy Martinez's remains last month. Good work! There's a chance the evidence we collected will lead to her killer. The cooperation of the Reservation Police with our unit is very encouraging. Meeting adjourned."

After the meeting Rick Tower strode over to me with just a trace of swagger in his step. Rick's a dedicated posse member, a lean 6'4" tall with an angular face softened by a light brown mustache that barely covers his upper lip. His dark blue eyes usually twinkle with good humor, but I've seen them turn an implacable steel gray when a case he is working on goes sour.

"Sunshine, you want to drive up to Whitewater with me?"

"That would be great, Rick. Thanks." Although I still wince when Rick calls me Sunshine, I don't make a big deal out of it.

My mother named me Sunshine in some ethereal moment of birthing meditation. I hated the name until that sweet summer night seven years ago when Sergeant John "Johnny" Morgan proposed. He sang, *You Are My Sunshine,* leaned his guitar against the fender of his patrol car, and asked me to marry him. When I said "yes", he pulled me into the black and white, let the siren roar, and set the lights flashing. He kissed me until I thought I was going to need CPR.

Johnny was the only one who dared call me Sunshine until he introduced me to his partner, Rick Tower. Rick is a sergeant in the department, a volunteer weapons trainer for the posse, and even now after Johnny's death he's continued to be my friend.

"Hey Sunshine. We got major kudos for the recovery last April. You did good lady!"

"It was a team effort, Rick. But yeah, we did good! Not often we get lucky after a year's gone by. I still wonder what happened out there."

"Me too, Sunshine. Me too."

Chapter 2

May 1998
Dry Springs Indian Reservation

Evening shadows and spring wild flowers cloaked the dunes. The soft purple intensity of desert verbenas concealed the dark stains soaking in to the sand. Lucy Martinez's footprints left a staggered trail away from the road to a sheltered place under the thick cover of a mesquite tree. A small owl emerged from his burrow to hunt his dinner and quickly flew away from the motionless form that had just collapsed next to the hole that led to his daylight habitat. In a last desperate move, the dying woman reached into the torn lining of her purse, removed a computer disc encased in plastic, and shoved it into the burrow. A gentle but persistent rain began to fall.

Two men jumped out of a blue van with the Lucky Aces Casino logo on the side panel. The passenger, dressed in a tan sport jacket and slacks, smoothed a few stray blonde hairs back in place and snarled angrily at the driver, a well-muscled Native American wearing jeans and a sweatshirt with a Lucky Aces Casino logo. "There's her car. She's around here somewhere. Find her! Search the car! I have to get that disc!"

"Make up your mind. You want me to look for her or search the car?"

"Shut up Jake. See if you can find her, I'll check the car."

"Yes sir, Mr. Harwin." Jake followed the footprints into the desert and came back ten minutes later shaking his head. "She's dead. I found her purse. No computer disc. Her driver's license says she's Lucy Martinez but she hired on at the casino as Lucy Ramirez. What's up man?"

"Never mind, asshole." Harwin opened the rear door and searched under the seat. "There's nothing in the car either," he growled angrily. "It has to be somewhere here."

"The woman's dead. She didn't have time to stash anything and she ain't talking. She don't have the frigging disc." Jake threw the purse on the back seat of the car.

"Jake, you saw the bitch snooping around the office. She came out, the disc's gone. You stupid shit! Why'd you shoot her before you found out what she did with it?"

"What'd yuh expect me to do?" Jake grumbled. "Anyways, whatever she was up to, she ain't up to it no more."

The tall man's face showed no emotion. "You left your keys to the office where she could find them."

Jake scowled aggressively, "How was I to know what she was gonna do?"

"Shut up muscle head! I have to think."

"You got no call to talk to me like that. My boss finds out you faked casino records and you'll…"

"You're right." The tall lanky man's eyes grew large and dark.

Jake saw the small snub nosed pistol. "Now … Mr. Harwin, I wouldn't …"

"Your boss won't find out." Harwin smiled ruthlessly at the trembling man and pulled the trigger.

He put Jake's body in the trunk of Lucy's car and drove it to the parking lot of an all-night grocery store, hitched a ride back to the van, and drove it back to the casino. Lucy slept lifelessly under the stars while the coyotes fed well.

Chapter 3

May 1998
State Capitol – Sacramento, California

The judge pinched his secretary's ample bosom and gave her the day off. He was visibly upset, his bloated face florid as he waited for his son to speak.

"Dad. I…"

"It's about time you called. I've been waiting all morning. Didn't you get my message?"

"Yeah, I…"

"Did you get the information?" The judge growled impatiently.

"Yeah, but I need more money."

"I'll see what I can do."

"You let me down the last time."

"Your stepmother controlled the money, in case you've forgotten." There was a short pause. "Without her help, I didn't have a chance in hell of getting reelected to the Senate," the judge reminded him. "Thank God I don't have to worry about the will of the people anymore."

"How is Agnes, anyway? Still pissed at me?" his son chuckled.

"You haven't exactly endeared yourself to her."

"Right. I offended my dear stepmother."

The judge spoke angrily. "You went to prison; almost wrecked my career."

"This time I saved it for you. Even Supreme Court judges can be recalled. Tell the governor the casino CEO is using casino money to fund political campaigns. I sent you a copy of the doctored disc to prove it."

"What about the originals?" The judge's voice was forceful.

"Don't worry. Nobody's going to find the originals."

"Once we prove the Indians are using casino money illegally, there's no way they can stop us."

"Dad, your damn proof is in the mail."

"How did you get it?"

"You don't want to know."

"Son, this is a secure line. Tell me what you did."

His son sneered, "Sure Dad. Thanks to me, the computer in the accounting office was suddenly hit with a virus. I substituted a bogus disc in the back-up files. It'll prove that a couple of the high mucky mucks are taking money from the casino and forcing employees to donate to your opponents' campaign funds. Even if the casino manager suspects the books were fixed there's no way to prove it. All you have to do is insist on an audit and the back-up disk with the fake records on it will take them down. They can't disprove the charges. Their computer has a new hard drive, and I set a little fire that destroyed the record books, so they'll have to rely on the back-up discs."

"Son, I hope you're right. The tribes must not get enough signatures for an initiative on the next ballot. The way things are going; Indian gaming down there in the desert could cut into our profits big time. My ass is grass if they succeed."

"Don't worry."

"Worry is all I do anymore."

"Dad, things got a little out of control. I have to get out of town for a while. I need cash."

"I heard rumors that you blew it. I heard that a couple of people were killed down there. You know anything about that?"

"The original disc won't show up. I guarantee it."

"You've given me reason not to trust you. Why should I believe you?"

"Looks like you don't have much choice."

"Son," the judge snarled menacingly, "I don't need to remind you where your money is coming from *now*. It wouldn't be a good idea to disappoint them."

Chapter 4

June 1998
Lucky Aces Casino

A dust devil swirled impetuously across the Lucky Aces parking lot, grabbed last night's flotsam and jetsam, whirled plastic bags and yesterday's newspapers in its windy column of dust, and tossed them gleefully into an early morning patron's shiny black convertible. I laughed, *Must be a lousy gambler, left the top down.* The desert whirlwind suddenly turned and spitefully blew a blast of sand in my face as I climbed out of my Toyota wagon.

Shit! I swiped at my eyes with the back of my hand. "Enough, okay?" Even the elements were slamming me. I took a tissue out of my purse and wiped away tears that had nothing to do with the dust devil that had already dissipated. *I'm losing it! Damn it!* I slammed the car door. *I can't take much more.* I mentally kicked myself and remembered the child I was supposed to be helping.

I worked as a counselor at a shelter for abused children. My mission this morning was to locate Lucy Martinez, who'd allegedly abandoned her ten year old son, Paulo. A social worker brought him to the shelter until a family member could be contacted. I was due to go off duty but my supervisor handed me the Martinez file. "Sunny, I'm short-handed. Can you take this one?"

I must have 'pushover' stamped on my forehead. "Sure. No problem."

I questioned the distraught boy. Between sobs he poured out his story. His father was in jail and he was afraid something terrible had happened to his mother. He said she'd taken a part-time job working as a dealer at the Lucky Aces Casino. She was supposed to work the previous night and return home the next morning, but she never came back. He'd waited all day for her, and in desperation, finally called 911.

When I asked him if he had any family he stopped crying. "My uncle Antonio. He'll help me."

"Antonio Martinez?" I remembered a benefit dinner for battered women that I helped to organize. He'd approached me, handsome, charismatic, and demanding. I was married at the time and told him so, but he'd affected me deeply. If I'd been single I would have responded differently. I shuddered involuntarily. "I think I know your uncle. Do you have a phone number for him?"

"Yes." Paulo gave me the number and I punched it in. I got voice mail and left a message for Antonio to call the shelter.

Paulo frowned. "My mom works for the Lucky Aces Casino," he added hopefully. "Maybe they know something."

I put a call through to the manager of the Lucky Aces Casino. He insisted that Lucy Martinez was not employed at the casino, but when I told him her maiden name was Ramirez he said, "Oh, I know who you want. Didn't show up for her shift or call in. Not like her at all. Haven't heard from her since day before yesterday."

"Would it be okay for me to talk to some of the people who work with her?"

"Sure, come on down. If you find out anything, let me know." He hesitated, "She hasn't picked up her paycheck."

I drove out to the Lucky Aces and found the manager, a thin Native American man in a three-piece suit and cowboy boots. A leather bolo tie fastened with a huge turquoise cabochon set in silver hung lazily around his neck. "Can I help you with something?"

"My name is Sunny Morgan. I talked to you earlier. You said you might have some information about Lucy Ramirez Martinez?"

"Yeah. Sarah, come over here for a minute."

"What ya want?"

"This lady's from the county. She wants to talk to you about Lucy." The manager turned to me, "Sarah might be able to help you," and then as though he had too much on his mind to be of any more help, he wandered away muttering to himself.

A short Native American woman almost as round as she was tall waddled over to me. "I'm Sarah."

"Sarah, my name's Sunny Morgan. I'm trying to find Lucy Ramirez Martinez. Is there anything you can tell me?"

"She's a good woman. Lives on the Rez near me. Helped me to get my job here. She said it was what a person did, not how they looked that mattered. Gave me the nerve to apply. I'm off welfare now because of her. I'll help if I can."

"Lucy's missing. No one's seen her since she left home to come to work here yesterday. Did she say anything to you? Was she worried about something?"

"Well, I'm not sure, but the last time I saw her she was just going off the morning shift. Must have been about three in the afternoon. Said she was scheduled to work a split shift but she might be late. Asked me if I'd cover for her. I told her I would." Sarah paused, "Lucy was talking kinda funny, like maybe she was upset about something. Said somebody was giving her a hard time but she was going to fix him."

"Did she mention any names, or say anything about why?"

"No, and I didn't ask her."

"Any idea why someone would give her a hard time?"

"Look, she was always asking questions. It's dangerous to ask stuff like that. She made a lot of people upset." Sarah whispered.

"What kind of questions? Who was upset?"

"She told me she thought someone here planted drugs on her husband but she'd found out something big; bigger than drugs."

"Did she tell you what?"

"No, just that it was big."

"Did she tell you anything that might help me find her?"

"Well... not really," Sarah turned around to see if anyone was listening and then continued in almost a whisper, "but I noticed her watching Jake, one of the bouncers here. Next thing you know Jake's dead in the trunk of Lucy's car. They found her purse but Lucy was nowhere around."

I was shocked. Why didn't the manager tell me about Lucy's car? "Who's in charge of the investigation?"

"The Rez cops and a couple of guys in suits were here asking us a lot of questions about money and election stuff. I know Lucy found out something. Maybe she got scared and took off, or maybe she's dead, too. I told her to carry some protection."

"Did she?"

"Lucy wouldn't never touch a gun, but I …"

"Sara, I'm here to help."

My offer to help didn't register. I recognized the blank stare. She continued, "Never you mind, Miss. Lucy's brother-in-law is here. Lucy 'called' him. He has the 'sight'. He'll find her."

"What do you mean, 'has the sight'?"

"I've already told you more than I should have." Sara's brief openness slammed down like a shutter on her face.

"Sarah…?"

"Look, I don't know anything. I have to get back to work. The boss is jumping all over everyone today." She glanced at the manager, frowned, and started to turn away.

"Sarah here's my card with a phone number where you can reach me. If you think of anything more, please call me."

The manager had his back to us. Sarah quickly pocketed the card. I watched her hurry back to her work station. She looked a little shaken and pointedly ignored me as she continued putting together the bingo packets for that night's customers. Sarah knew more than she was willing to tell me, of that I was sure, but she'd put me out of her mind. Pride in her job glowed on her face as she sat down at her work station.

A tall Native American in a fringed leather jacket and stone-washed jeans strode purposefully across the casino floor. He appeared to be in his mid-forties; his long black hair was lightly streaked with gray and worn in two braids bound with leather thongs. He smiled but his hazel eyes burned into mine. "Remember me? Antonio Martinez. You're Sunny, Sunny Morgan. I got your message about Paulo," his demeanor was earnest, his voice deep and throaty with emotion. "I *knew* you would be here."

"Antonio?" I wanted to turn away from him and run out of the casino, but I was held in place like a deer mesmerized by a mountain lion's gaze. He stared at me for a few seconds then turned and walked out of the casino.

In the next moment, it was *déjà vu* time. A man walked up to me. He could have been Antonio, but his hair was pulled back in a ponytail instead of braids, and there was a frown on his face instead of a smile. "My name's Daniel Martinez. I have to talk to you.

Antonio said you were looking for Lucy. She's my sister-in-law. My nephew, Paulo, reported her missing."

I felt like I had fallen into the middle of somebody else's movie. "Yes. I'm looking for Lucy."

Daniel continued, "The police told me that people often choose to disappear without telling their families where they're going, but not Lucy. They insinuated she was involved with the murder of a man who worked for the casino. Not true! I *know*. Besides, she'd never abandon her son. She's dead. Her blood was found in the car she was driving. The problem is, the car was registered to me, and now the authorities won't release my nephew into my custody."

"Mr. Martinez, I'll check into this. We always try to keep families together."

"I understand, but my brother, Antonio, got custody of Paulo. This time your agency made a mistake. Antonio will take him just to spite me. He's already poisoned the boy's mind against me."

"I'm sure the agency checked him out thoroughly before deciding to release your nephew into his custody."

"I've seen Lucy crying on the other side. She begged *me* to take care of her son and help her find peace."

I'd heard denial from family members many times, but there was a twist to this I hadn't heard before. Antonio, the evil twin? I didn't think so. The look on my face must have given me away. "I ... okay, tell me what you know." My disbelief was obvious.

"Antonio isn't the only one with power." Daniel seemed almost embarrassed. "I have walked in the spirit world as well. I know you are in pain. You're alone now. I hear a gunshot. I see a man in uniform. His life's blood is flowing out of him. I see him in the hospital His spirit is no longer with him. You chose to let his body go to greet his spirit. This was painful for you. Now you need to find peace in your life. There is someone who is helping you because he feels responsible for your loss. I will show you a path to walk so that you can heal yourself."

I was reeling. "That wasn't what I asked. I asked what you know about Lucy Martinez!"

"I *know* you will find out what happened to her. Your life and mine are entwined by sorrows from the past, and challenges yet to come. I saw your face in a vision. We have much to do. Our journey together has just begun."

I heard what he said, but I couldn't make sense of it. It wasn't rational. He was demanding that I begin some kind of journey I didn't want with someone I didn't know. Daniel's anger with Antonio still contorted his face even as he was speaking to me. I was skeptical and frightened about what Daniel said he *saw*. Visions aren't my thing, but how could he have known about Johnny?

"Are you crazy?" I flatly rejected what he said. "I have a job to do and you're not helping." Abruptly, I escaped from Daniel and ran out of the casino.

A few days later Daniel called the shelter.

"Ms. Morgan, I didn't mean to alarm you when we met at the casino. I came to the casino to find out what happened to my sister-in-law." He paused, "I'm the manager of the Marietta Ranch. I've been looking for someone to order supplies and keep the ranch records. You are in the market for another job, aren't you?" he chuckled. " Just intuition."

I was still angry about Johnny's death and overwhelmed with guilt. I didn't have any compassion left inside me to give to the women and children who came to the shelter. Something else, anything else, sounded good. This time I didn't even question how Daniel *knew*.

"You've got that right. I need a change, but …"

"Give it a try. You do love horses. The pay isn't great, but you'll live on the ranch. No rent and animals are allowed."

"I have a BA in psychology. I don't think that qualifies me to take on the business end of a horse ranch."

"Don't worry about it. You'll do fine."

I thought for a moment. "I must be out of my mind, but I'll give it a try."

A week later I got a letter from the owners of the Marietta Ranch. I was to start work immediately. They'd hired me based solely on Daniel's recommendation. I turned in my resignation at the shelter.

After checking out my future home, I stored most of my furniture, rented a small U-Haul truck, filled it with a few necessary possessions, coaxed my cat Chowder into her carrier, and drove to the ranch. There wasn't room in the truck cab for Shadow, a huge Doberman-Rottweiler mix, but Rick promised to feed her that night and bring her over to the ranch in the morning. Shadow was Johnny's dog, but now she and I learned to maintain an uneasy truce. She had to eat and I couldn't bear to take her to the pound.

When I arrived at the Marietta Ranch I was filled with second thoughts. The double-wide mobile home that the owners provided looked just like the one I grew up in. It was even the same awful salmon color. I found the packing box with my sheets, made the bed, and curled up around a body pillow. It didn't replace a warm, loving partner but it was all I had. Even Chowder refused to stay on the bed with me. That night I sobbed into my pillow. *What have I done?*

The next morning Daniel brought me the *Desert Sun* newspaper. "You might be interested in this." He'd folded the paper to an article about some horses that needed a new home.

On impulse I called the number listed in the paper and drove out to see them. One of the horses lifted his head, snorted, and trotted over to me. An old cowboy greeted me, spurs jangling. "This here's Max. He's been rode hard and put up wet. My name's Tex."

I could see that Max had been badly mistreated, but I knew his spirit was still very much alive. "How'd he end up here?"

The wrangler drawled, "Li'l lady, we rescued this here fella from a small corral in the high desert. He was 'most starved to death. You got a place to keep him?"

A shiver went through me. I thought about what Daniel had said. "Uh, yes. I'm living on the Marietta Ranch. I … yes, Tex. I do have a place to keep him."

"That the ranch where Daniel Martinez works?"

"Yes."

"That's all the references this outfit wants, and this here hoss sure do need a home."

I didn't realize it at first, but I needed Max more than he needed me. The Horse Rescue Mission trailered him over to the Marietta Ranch that afternoon.

I spent every spare moment brushing him and feeding him a special mix of grains that Laura Kinston, the ranch veterinarian, recommended. He gained weight and his coat glistened. On my days off I rode him up the Lost Mine Canyon behind the ranch. Max was good company. He didn't ask for much, just pasture, hay, water, and exercise. Oats, bran, and a salt lick were extras as far as Max was concerned. As soon as he was fit, Rick convinced me to join the posse.

Chapter 5

Marietta Ranch

Daniel was my boss, but much to my consternation, he continued to treat me as his student. He insisted that I learn more about the history of the Cahuilla Indian people. One Saturday about a month after I started working at the Marietta, Daniel asked me to go with him to a small museum run by the local historical society.

We got to the museum just as it opened. The elderly lady at the desk asked for a two dollar donation, and offered to have a docent take us through the museum. Daniel declined and escorted me to a small exhibit of Indian artifacts. There was a painting of an Indian woman on the wall.

Daniel whispered, "That's my mother."

The plaque beneath the painting read, *Evana Martinez, Cahuilla Medicine Woman.*

I admired the ollas, large decorated clay pots with rounded bottoms and narrow necks. "They're so beautiful. How did the people manage to get that shape? They didn't have pottery wheels then, did they?"

Daniel spoke with pride. "The ollas were made by coiling long ropes of clay and the sides smoothed with a stone."

"Daniel, they're incredible."

"Look closely. Do you see those fingerprints?"

"Yes."

"They were embedded in clay by the person who made that olla over 200 years ago." Daniel lovingly put his hands on one of the smaller ollas and turned to me. "Sunny, this one was taken from an Indian campsite by pot hunters who didn't understand the importance of our history."

"How did it end up in a museum?

Daniel ignored my question. "When I touch this olla, I see a woman filling it with chia seeds and sealing the top with a round pottery plug. It's covered with a net woven from yucca fiber for carrying. She's storing food for the long journey to their summer camp in the Santa Rosa Mountains.

I was entranced. "That's beautiful!"

Daniel's eyes shimmered. He continued as though he hadn't heard me. "Her husband is waiting impatiently and two round-faced children are playing nearby. She's smiling at me from across the barriers of time."

Daniel turned to me. His eyes returned to normal.

"Did you really see that woman?"

"Yes, like a video in my mind."

It still makes me nervous when he does that. I changed the subject and asked him if we could see some of the other exhibits.

Daniel shrugged and put his arm around me. "I'm not really interested in the pioneer artifacts." He glanced at me and laughed at my surprise. "Not that they aren't important, but the pioneers aren't on the endangered species list." He became more serious when he pointed out an exhibit of baskets protected behind glass. "But if it weren't for the white settlers, those baskets wouldn't even be here. They valued beauty even though they didn't value the people who created it."

"Daniel, I don't understand."

"Do you see the tightly woven rattlesnake design on that basket?"

"Yes, Daniel, it's beautifully done. The black and yellow colors and the intricate design against the natural color of the basket are amazing."

"Sunny, the Cahuilla woman who made that basket was an outstanding artist. Can't you see the irony of the value placed on what they created and the indifference to the person who was the artisan?"

"I never thought of it that way before." Daniel put his hand on the small of my back and guided me out of the museum. His gentle touch surprised me and I found myself thinking about how much I enjoyed sharing time with him.

Chapter 6

May 1999
Marietta Ranch

I'd been on the posse almost a year and had been on several rescues. When Rick asked me to go on a search and recovery operation, I jumped at the chance.

"Sunny, I think we may have found Lucy Martinez's remains. You were involved in her case, weren't you? Do you have time to be in on the recovery? We aren't going to use the horses; it's strictly a foot soldier operation, but it would be good experience for you."

"Sure!" That case troubled me for a lot of reasons; not the least of which was the connection with Daniel and his belief that I would find out what happened to his sister-in-law. "I guess Max won't mind staying home this once, and I could use some exercise. Are they sure it's Lucy's remains?"

"Not a hundred percent. It's been nearly a year since she disappeared, but a bracelet that matches the description of the one she was wearing when she disappeared was found near some of the bones. Coyotes have probably spread pieces of her skeleton all over."

"Sounds gruesome."

"Sunshine, get over it. If it's her remains, the family deserves to know, and she deserves a proper burial. Maybe we can finally determine what happened to her."

"I know, it's just … how did they find …?"

"A photographer stopped by the side of the road up near the reservation. He found some bones, the bracelet, and a few tattered clothes. Called 911 on his cell phone."

"Have you called Daniel? Lucy was his sister-in-law, after all. He's been waiting a long time for news."

"No, I haven't called Daniel." Rick gave me an odd look. "We're going to wait until we're sure."

"I understand. Should I drive out there?"

"No, I'll pick you up in about an hour."

"Okay, I'll leave the gate unlocked."

Precisely 60 minutes later Rick drove up in his truck, stomped up to the porch, and banged on the door. He had a scowl on his face that would make half the criminal population in the desert put their hands in the air. "Rick, what's wrong?"

"It's always the same. Politics! The Rez police and the department are arguing about jurisdiction. Damn it! We were all set to go. I wish somebody would figure it out. Forget the search, it was called off. The reservation cops are on it." He looked like a kid who'd just been grounded for something he didn't do.

"I'm sorry Rick; I know how you must feel. Let's get out of here. There's a new mare that just came in from one of the other ranches. She needs some exercise. She's a little skittish, but you'll enjoy riding her."

"You got it, Sunshine!" Rick smiled for the first time since he knocked on the door. "Let's do it."

"I want to call Daniel first."

"Yeah, he really should know. I don't have a problem with that." I could tell that he did.

I was reaching for the phone when it rang. "Hello?"

"This is Daniel. Sunny, I had to call you."

Shivers went up and down my spine. "God! Daniel! I was just going to call you."

"I've had a feeling all day that something important is about to happen. Talk to me! What's happened?"

"Daniel, Rick is here. He thinks Lucy's remains have been found. The posse was called out to search and recover whatever we could, but the Reservation Police have denied us access to the area."

"Not to worry, Sunny. Give me a couple of hours. I have a few people to call. My dear brother Antonio's fingers are stirring this pot. I'm not going to let him stop me from finding out what happened to Lucy. I'll call you after eight tonight. By the way, go ahead and take that ride. It will do you good."

Damn! He did it again! I put down the phone with a shudder. "Rick, let's saddle up the horses and get the flock out of here!" I clomped down to the pasture in my dusty boots and gave Max a quick brush. He nuzzled me and almost knocked me over as I threw the saddle blanket on. "Max, quit it!"

"Sunshine, that's a fine Indian blanket. Where'd you get it?"

I snapped at Rick, "Don't remember." I didn't tell him that it was the only legacy that my father left me. "Just something I picked up somewhere." Now we were both in a bad mood.

The air smelled of rain that had evaporated long before it could fall to earth. We rode for about an hour when I decided to ask Rick about Daniel. "What do you know about Daniel Martinez?"

He glanced at me with a disgruntled sneer. "Why so interested?"

"Daniel says things that confuse me. It's unnerving when he knows more about me than he should. I haven't figured out what's up with him."

"Sunshine ..."

"Rick, I really need to know."

Rick raised one eyebrow and thoughtfully stroked his light brown mustache. "I can tell you what I've heard around the station. Word is that Daniel and his brothers are descendants of witch doctors."

"You mean shaman?"

"Yeah," He took a deep breath as though he was trying to put the latest frustration out of his mind. "Daniel's mother was a Cahuilla Indian who was a ..." Rick thought for a second, "medicine woman. She married Daniel's father much against the wishes of both their families. He was the only son of a wealthy family and marrying an Indian woman was a huge scandal."

"Times have changed. I don't think anyone would even blink now."

Rick shook his head and said, "To be honest with you, I don't think things have really changed that much. The family disowned Daniel's father when he married. It was whispered that Daniel's mother put a spell on the family. Not everyone believed it, but some did. Both his parents died in a fire."

"I didn't know about that."

"Arson, maybe even murder, was suspected, but no one was ever arrested. Daniel, Antonio, and their younger brother Michael were just boys at the time."

"That's terrible."

"It left its mark on the three brothers. Daniel put it behind him and went on to college. I have to give him credit for that. His twin brother, Antonio, stayed on the reservation. I don't know much about him. Michael's heavy into radical politics from what I hear. Lucy Ramirez was a beautiful girl. I went to school with her. Never understood why she married him. Michael's been arrested more than once for disturbing the peace; nothing serious until he was arrested for physically abusing his wife. When push came to shove ..." Rick glanced at me to see if I would at least smile. I didn't. Rick grimaced. "She refused to press charges. She even denied that Michael had ever laid a hand on her. It's always the same."

"Rick, there's nothing funny about being battered!"

"I didn't mean that. There wasn't any proof that he ever hurt her. The source remained anonymous." Rick shrugged knowingly. "Come on Sunshine. I was just trying ..."

"I know, Rick. It's just not funny."

Rick wanted to make his point but he decided to let it go. "We got Michael Martinez anyway. Drugs."

I remembered my conversation with Sarah at the casino. "Did Lucy say anything?"

"Yeah, she denied that Michael ever used meth. But she's his wife."

"And now she's probably dead. Could there be a connection?"

Rick shook his head. "I wasn't surprised when Lucy 'disappeared'. Two Indian activists died under mysterious circumstances, like a bullet in the back of the head. Lucy was as much into tribal politics as Michael."

"So what happened to Michael?"

"He was demonstrating against some compost company. Now that I think about it, it was just before Lucy disappeared. We were tipped off. Found methamphetamine on him. He claimed it wasn't his but went down."

"Could someone have planted it?"

"Sunshine, you're always for the underdog, right or wrong."

"I read about the backers of that composting scheme. They could have ..."

"I give …" Rick waved both his hands in the air nearly dropping the reins. "Hey, I didn't get involved in that mess."

I paid no attention to his theatrics. "Rick, I remember now. They were trucking in human waste from Los Angeles. There was a huge demonstration. Michael Martinez was one of the organizers."

"Yeah … but he went to jail for possession of an illegal substance. Besides Sunshine, there are legal ways to handle disputes. Anyway, the weird thing is that Antonio Martinez was a partner in the company. Go figure."

"What about Antonio?"

"If there's money to be made, he's in the middle of it." Rick glanced at me. "Helped to get the compost company to invest on Indian land; mainly his. Michael claimed the ground water was being compromised. Antonio denied it. Brother against brother. Never understood that one."

"And Daniel?"

Rick glowered, "Never talked to him. He stayed out of tribal political stuff as far as I know. He's *assisted* our department with criminal cases that involve his people. Uses his big time education to get them off. Didn't work that time."

"Rick!" I was astonished by the venom in his voice. "Daniel has visions like the old time shamans. He's told me many stories about the Great Spirit and the messages and warnings that different animals bring, and I don't think he thinks of them as fantasy. He cares about what happens to the earth."

Rick had no patience for anything mystical. "Don't listen to any of that crap; nothing but smoke and mirrors. Old Indian myths. And besides, it's Antonio who has the rep for being a shaman, not Daniel. One of the deputies interviewed Antonio after the demonstration. There was no love lost among those brothers. Antonio claimed that Michael's a doper and Daniel's a sham not a shaman. According to Antonio, Daniel gets his psychic garbage from books."

I was about to come to Daniel's defense again, but Rick's disclosures stopped me cold. I kicked Max in the flanks and loped ahead. Rick caught up with me. "Come on Sunshine! Don't get me wrong. I'm not prejudiced."

"Damn it, Rick!" I was incensed. "Daniel has a master's degree in anthropology. He volunteers a lot of time at the reservation community center and teaches a class for the Indian kids who want to learn the Cahuilla language. He's one of the good guys! Most of the elders who spoke the language are dead. Daniel is encouraging the young people to learn. That's a good thing. Don't you think so?"

"Yeah, if you say so, but this other stuff ..." Rick growled. "He's just putting you on with that weird nonsense. If you didn't want to hear what I had to say, you shouldn't have asked."

I couldn't decide if Rick was trying to be honest about his feelings or if he was jealous of Daniel. Our friendship sometimes gets troublesome and confusing.

Rick is separated from his wife, but he's never mentioned wanting a divorce, and he's never made a move on me. He says she goes from one bad relationship to another almost as often as she changes the color of her hair. He shrugs it off. "We got married to young."

We rode in silence for a while. What Rick told me about Daniel raised more questions than it answered.

"Sunny," Rick said hesitantly, "I didn't mean to upset you."

"I know."

When we got back to the ranch there was a message on the answering machine from Daniel. "Sunny, please have Rick call me at home. It's urgent."

I could tell that Rick wasn't pleased but he placed the call. I listened to the conversation on our end but all I heard was, "Okay. All right. Yes, I'll arrange it." Rick put the portable phone back on the charger.

"Sunny, I don't know how Daniel did it, but the posse will be cooperating with the Reservation Police to recover Lucy's remains. I'll pick you up at six in the morning."

Chapter 7

May 1999
Dry Springs Indian Reservation

Rick arrived early and we shared a hot cup of coffee before heading out under the cloudless blue skies of a spring morning. This wasn't a practice recovery this time. It was the real thing.

There were two teams already on the scene; one was using dogs. One of the "ground pounders", an expert tracker from the Reservation Police, gave us the initial briefing.

"Deputy Tower, I'm Sergeant Benjamin Fox. Call me Ben. Thanks for bringing your people out. I know you're used to working mounted, but I'm sure you know horses could destroy evidence. It's going to be tough enough as it is. I'll show you what we have." He held up a human jawbone. "This is the largest piece we have recovered so far. We'll be able to confirm identification now. What you're looking for may look like small, dry, brown sticks. The bones may be hidden under dense brush or covered by sand. We're going to have your team do a line search to the left of that mesquite tree. If any of you need a drag stick, there are some extras in our van."

Rick straightened his six-foot, four-inch tall frame and glared at the sergeant. "Thanks, but we brought our own equipment." Under his breath he grumbled, "Pompous asshole."

The five-foot, eleven-inch tall sergeant ignored the insult. He spoke quietly, "Well …" he paused, "Good. Get your people started."

We opened our packs and took out our Popsicle sticks and clothespins. Benjamin Fox took off his Nike baseball cap and scratched his head. "What in the name of the Great Spirit is that?"

Rick scowled defensively. "Clip the clothespins to the stick, attach your flagging tape and you have quick and easy markers for evidence.

Ben Fox slapped his cap against his knee producing a small cloud of dust. "That's a great idea."

Ricks jaws were clenched tight, but when he realized Fox's praise was genuine he grinned, "Yep."

We hoisted the rest of our equipment out of the Sheriff Posse van and formed a line across the sector where Fox had told us to search. Drag sticks work well when searching for evidence that is covered by debris or sand. I had only been searching for about fifteen minutes when I felt my stick hit something solid. I bent down and dug a little into the soft sand. It was a plastic case with a computer disc in it. Rick was next to me about twelve feet away. "Rick, I think I found something. It's not a bone, but look at this."

"Sunny, flag that puppy. Its location may be important. We'll come back with Sergeant Fox and check it out. You can tell it's been out here for a while. I wonder if the disc is still good."

We recovered enough to identify the remains as Lucy Martinez. The disc was sent to the lab for further examination. Ben and Rick shook hands and promised to assist each other in the future. A substantial breakthrough in cooperation between the Sheriff's Department and the Reservation Police began that day.

Lucy's remains were not buried right away though. Daniel asked me to attend Lucy's wake. I was afraid that his people wouldn't accept me, but I promised I would come out of respect for Lucy and her family. I followed Daniel's directions to a rectangular structure built with mesquite limbs and branches that were mudded over. It was almost hidden in the giant mesquite trees which surrounded it. I searched desperately through the crowd of people for Daniel. In the early morning light, I saw him walking across the dusty road toward the ceremonial house.

"Wait! Daniel!" I ran toward him and touched his arm. He turned his face toward me. It was Daniel, but it wasn't.

"You! What are you doing here?!"

"Daniel?"

"Oh," he sneered, "it's because of my dear brother that you are here. You have no right to be here. Daniel never should have asked you to come."

It was Antonio. He scowled at me but I retorted angrily. "I'm here. I was invited and I wanted to be here. Where's Daniel?"

Antonio raised his arm and pointed a long-nailed finger toward the ceremonial house. "He's over there talking to the dancers. He's valiantly trying to turn this farce into a *spiritual event.* What would he, my dear college-educated brother, know of such things?"

I was terrified. "Antonio, I ..."

"Yes. You ..." He stalked away muttering to himself.

I shuddered at the frightening force of his words and ran toward the dancers, colliding into Daniel. "Oh Daniel. I ..."

"Sunny, what's the matter? Your face is as pale as the moon in daylight."

"Antonio. He ... I thought it was you."

"My twin brother. He enjoys frightening people. Put him out of your mind. We are here to honor my sister-in-law." He put his arm around me and with his hand at the small of my back, guided me into the ceremonial house.

"I'm sorry I couldn't meet you, Sunny. The dancers have come all the way from Arizona to honor Lucy. I had to welcome them. My people have forgotten the dances. It is my dream to teach them to respect their heritage. We, the Cahuilla, were a mighty nation and had trade with many other tribes once. Now we depend on others to help us find our heritage."

"Daniel ..."

"Don't feel sorry for us Sunny. There's a rising of spirit that flows through all the peoples. We will learn of our father's truths again. It isn't too late."

The celebration of Lucy's life and the sadness of her death continued all that day and until the early morning hours of the next.

Outside the ceremonial house tables were loaded with traditional foods for the mourners. The next morning all those who still remained raised their arms and rushed about chasing away the spirits so they would not linger here on earth to make mischief.

Daniel walked me back to my old Toyota. "Sunny, I am pleased that you came. Someday I will tell you more. Not now."

A giant white owl flew in front of my car and out of sight as I drove away from that place. I felt a fullness of spirit, a true good-bye to a woman I never knew.

Chapter 8

July 11, 1999
Marietta Ranch

It was almost dark when I finished brushing Max after a long, dusty ride looking for signs of a legendary gold mine that was supposed to exist somewhere near the mesa at the end of the canyon behind the ranch. I walked toward my trailer and saw a black Mercedes parked in front. I recognized the slender five-foot, four-inch form of the woman hurrying toward me. She was wearing a pristine white tennis outfit, her short blonde hair tucked under a smart white beret. I wondered how she could look so cool and unrumpled this time of year. I swear that woman doesn't even sweat.

"Hey Sunny, I hoped you'd be home. Is that spooky Indian around?"

Not a good beginning. "Caroline, Daniel's a medicine man and he's my friend. He just lost someone he loved and he's gone to meditate in the mountains."

"Whatever. He gives me the willies." She shivered. "I have to talk to you."

I bit my tongue. "What's up? I thought we were going to get together next weekend."

"Sunny, you have to do me a favor."

Caroline never asks, she demands. I tried to keep a smile on my face. "I'll help if I can."

"Carrie has to stay with you for a while. I've got major problems at home. Carrie doesn't need to be upset. She's been doing so well. I'll bring her over in the morning."

"There's a posse training set up for this weekend."

"You have to help!" Caroline screeched. The cool look disappeared and bright red patches showed through her carefully applied makeup. I took a deep breath. "You can bring her over

Monday morning. You know I enjoy having her stay with me, but I have a posse exercise this weekend."

"But, Sunny…"

"I won't be here this weekend." I'd learned the hard way not to give in to Caroline's whining. "Bring her over Monday morning."

"Can't you cancel?"

"No. This training's mandatory." I repeated firmly, "Monday."

Caroline's face turned several shades of red. "It would help if she could stay over the weekend while I get things sorted out."

"Monday, Caroline. First thing. Okay?"

"Last time you were developing your spiritual self with that … that medicine man and now it's the posse. Carrie needs your help!"

Caroline's eleven year old daughter Carrie often stayed with me while Caroline went on buying trips for her boutique. Carrie's IQ was off the top, but she'd been diagnosed with ADHD when she was a kindergartner; unusual for a girl, and Caroline's secret pain.

"Want to talk?"

Caroline was sulking. I recognized the pout on her face. "Can't right now. I thought I could count on you. There's some bad stuff happening and I need Carrie safely tucked away." She began to sulk. "Don't trouble yourself. Maybe everything will work out." Caroline's tears threatened to overflow. She knows how to make me feel guilty; pushes every button trying to make me give in. "Are you sure you don't want to tell me what's going on?"

"Do you have the name of a good hit man?" The tears disappeared as quickly as they arrived. "No, I don't mean that. Sunny, I'm not even sure what I'm going to do." Caroline tried to smile.

"Okay, no questions, but I really can't take Carrie until Monday." I wasn't going to change my plans on such short notice and I wasn't going to get sucked in on another one of Caroline's crises unless it was a real emergency. "After this weekend I'll be happy to have Carrie stay with me for as long as you need. I'll make up the sofa bed in the living room."

Caroline shook her head. "I have to go."

"I'll be back Sunday night. I'll call you."

"Right." She pursed her bright red lips. "If it isn't too much trouble." She got back into the Mercedes and sent gravel flying all the way to the gate.

It didn't do any good to worry. Caroline's business often takes her away on buying trips and she needs someone to ride herd on Carrie, but usually she just wants a day away from her family. I remembered her last crisis. She begged me to take Carrie because she wanted to have her hair done for a charity gala. Carrie is hyperactive, diagnosed with Attention Deficit Hyperactivity Disorder. Caroline was afraid Carrie couldn't sit still at the beauty salon. All she had to do was let Carrie get her hair done too. I shook my head. Caroline Costa always has emergencies of one kind or another. She draws small troubles like a magnet does iron and then she sends Carrie to me. I know Caroline loves her daughter dearly, but somehow her lifestyle keeps getting in the way. I don't think about it too much. I'm used to being a surrogate mom. I need Carrie in my life.

I watched Caroline drive out the gate and then walked into the trailer. Memories of my first encounter with Caroline flooded back. It was my first real job that summer of 1981. I was working at a stable in the mountains. I had to muck out a lot of stalls, but when business was slow, I got to exercise the horses. Most of them were old pluggers, but in my mind I was racing with the wind in my hair and my troubles at my back.

I discovered a profound peace on those mountain trails. I could forget the terror of my childhood years when I lay crying in my room listening to the drunken, knock-down screaming fights between my mother and her boyfriends. She threw me out of the house the summer before my freshman year in high school when she caught her latest boyfriend grabbing at my breasts and trying to kiss me.

One of the counselors at the shelter arranged a job for me at the Santa Rosa Stables and my love affair with horses began. I spent the next four school years with my grandparents and summers living in the mountains. Monte Frendle, the owner of Santa Rosa Stables, knew why people always asked for me to be their trail guide. I made sure that they had a good time and still came back in one piece. That kept Monte happy and I always had a job at the stables if I wanted it.

The summer of my senior year in high school Monte's niece, Caroline, came to spend the summer in the mountains. She was a city girl but she thought she knew everything there was to know about horses. We'd taken two of the liveliest horses from the stable. Carline was riding Buck, a buckskin gelding with a bad habit of shying at the slightest excuse, and I was riding Thunder, a 16 hands tall, shiny black except for a crooked white blaze that looked like a lightning streak. As long as Thunder was in the lead he was a perfect gentleman but if any horse ever got ahead of him he was hard to control. He'd tossed me once but after that I was prepared for his quirks.

Caroline decided she wanted to ride up to the Tahquitz Peak ranger station. In the first ten minutes Caroline informed me that a mare and a gelding were the same thing and I knew I was in for a long day. I decided to have a little fun with Miss know-it-all. I told Caroline about the handsome ranger that worked at the ranger station. What she didn't know was that the ranger was at least 50 years old. That seemed ancient to me back then.

After about an hour of hard riding up the switchbacks listening to Carline's continuous know-it-all babbling, we came to a spot that was relatively level and stopped to rest the horses.

Caroline complained, "I'm so hungry I could eat a rabid skunk!"

By that time I would have liked to see her do just that, but I'd packed peanut butter sandwiches and apples. "We've got better grub in the saddlebags."

"Well, let's eat!"

When I suggested we wait until we got up to the ranger's station she pursed her lips and shrieked, "I mean right now."

It was easier to let her have her own way than listen to her complain. I uncoiled the lead ropes, clipped them to the halters, and was about to tie Caroline's horse to a small pine tree.

"Give me the rope! I can take care of my own horse! You don't know everything."

"I don't know what your problem is." I handed the lead rope to Caroline. Usually I just loosen the cinch on the saddle to give the horse room to breathe, but Caroline wanted to stretch out for our afternoon picnic using a saddle as a pillow, something she'd seen in a movie, so I took the saddles off and put the sweaty blankets wet-side up over a manzanita bush; anything to keep the boss's niece happy or at least quiet.

We ate the apples and sandwiches, drank spring water from our canteens, and stretched out in the shade of a large boulder. Caroline had just finished brushing her hair and was putting on fresh lipstick to impress the ranger when that skunk she wanted to eat strolled out of the bushes.

Caroline screamed and spooked the horses. Buck pulled back and the rope and came loose. I'd tied Thunder to a pine tree using a bowline knot that Monte had taught me and even though my horse was pulling hard the rope stayed tied. Buck reared. I grabbed the lead rope but Buck pulled it from my hands and galloped down the switchbacks dragging the rope. He tripped on it, stumbled, and then disappeared from sight.

"Oh my God Sunny, we're stranded! We'll die out here! Nobody will ever find our bodies! We'll get eaten by mountain lions!" Caroline was really getting into it.

"Shut up!" I'd had all I could take of her hysterics. "No one's going to be eaten."

I just stood there for a minute shaking my head. Thunder could pack everything out of there. I put the saddle on, cinched it down tight, and put the other blanket and saddle on top. Then I slung the canteens on the saddle horn and tied Buck's bridle and saddlebags on behind the cantle. Caroline would have to hold on to the extra saddle to make sure it didn't slip off, but it was workable.

"Leave that stuff here!" Caroline ordered imperiously. "We can ride double. Uncle Monte wouldn't want me to have to walk all the way back to the stable."

"Caroline, I'm not leaving our gear. You walk along beside the horse and make sure your saddle doesn't fall off."

Thunder was nervous and wanted to follow Buck, but I soothed him with soft words and stroked his neck before I put the bridle back on to have more control. Then I picked up the lead rope and started the long walk back to the stables. Caroline started whining again. "I'm going to get stepped on by that four-legged monster of yours! We don't have any water! We're going to die! It's all your fault! Uncle Monte's going to fire you."

I wished I could find a mountain lion with enough appetite to eat Caroline. I wished I'd worn hiking shoes instead of my fancy cowboy boots.

Monte was brushing Buck when we arrived at the stables. He took one look and started laughing at the sight of the two of us limping back to the stables with a mountain of gear pile on one horse. I was tire and covered with dust but I'll never forget Monte's face when Caroline started ranting about how incompetent I was.

"Caroline," he said, chuckling. "You're lucky you were with my top hand. I would've put you over my knee and spanked you." Caroline walked off in a huff, but later on that evening she came back and apologized. "Sunny, I'm sorry. Thanks for getting us out of there."

"No problem. It's my job."

I just thought it wouldn't be a problem That September when I opened my dorm room door at UC Santa Barbara, I found my computer-assigned roommate had already arrived. There was Caroline hanging her clothes on both sides of the one small closet. I groaned to myself, "This is going to be a long year."

Caroline saw the dismay on my face. "I'm so glad you're my roommate," she gushed.

"She never let me forget our wild ride up the trail to Tahquitz Peak. Whenever she needed my help she'd quip, "When you save a life you're responsible for it."

Chapter 9

June 1998
Agua Grande Indian Reservation

The dust billowed around Daniel's truck as he drove into the Agua Grande Indian Reservation. He passed the community center, the only brick building on the "Rez". There was no grass, no flowers, only dirt and weeds. The center looked abandoned as though no one had been there in months. Daniel turned left at a large mesquite clump and parked next to a cannibalized '57 Cadillac. The rusted shell served as a home for a non-descript brown dog, her dugs almost dragging on the ground, and the one surviving pup from a litter of eight. The pup wriggled out to greet Daniel but the bitch pulled her tail between her legs, growling as she retreated into her metallic den.

Antonio Martinez was relaxing under a palm frond ramada supported by mesquite limb poles. He didn't get up but let Daniel come to him. He sneered, "Hello brother." He held up a glistening bottle of beer. "Want a Corona?"

"No." Daniel glanced around at the collection of animal skulls that his brother had attached to the poles. "Tony," Daniel acknowledged, "Where's Paulo?"

"Paulo's meditating at the moment. He can't see you now." Antonio grinned. "I'm impressed that you had the courage to visit me."

Daniel swallowed the taste of bile on his tongue. Paulo's placement would have to wait for another day. "Tony, I'm here to warn you. Leave Mary alone. She doesn't want to see you again."

"You!" Antonio laughed spitefully. "You came to warn me! How thoughtful dear brother. If Mary doesn't want to see me, she can speak for herself ... or ... is it you who doesn't want me around your precious woman?"

Daniel continued, "Tony, no good can come from what you are planning."

"Oh, now the college graduate wants to educate his ignorant red brother. And what do you know of my plans?"

Daniel straightened his powerful body to its full height, "I *know!*"

Antonio spit on the ground, "And did you learn it from your books, brother? Remember how you betrayed me? Those books ..."

"No, Tony, not from books; from the heart. I beg you." Daniel's entreaty was passionate, "What you are doing isn't good for our people."

"And what you did? That was good for our people?"

"I made amends for that. You have to stop this horror you sent forth!"

"And..." Tony paused, "what do *you* propose to do about it?"

"I will attempt to stop you."

"Not even I can prevent what is to come." Antonio's eyes darkened. "Daniel, my womb mate, you may think you have powers..." Antonio paused again and grinned horribly, "but you haven't the vaguest notion of what you're attempting. You have no idea in your limited realm of what danger you are subjecting those you care about. I strongly suggest that you leave voluntarily before I have to forcibly remove you from my presence."

"Good will overcome evil, Antonio. You have chosen a dark path and you will not prevail." Daniel was beginning to sweat.

"You are not without blame." Antonio motioned to Daniel with a crow's feather. "I think you'd better go now while you still can."

Daniel retreated a few feet and then staggered to his truck. The brown bitch snarled banefully at his heels. He could hear Antonio's barking laughter ringing in his ears as he backed the truck out of the driveway. He spoke calmly, "It's not over brother. You will not win in the end."

Daniel looked in his rear view mirror. A scrawny coyote was loping along behind the truck and veered off as Daniel turned onto the main road out of the reservation.

Chapter 10

July 1998

Daniel invited Rick and me to explore a cove above Lake Cahuilla and share a desert picnic with him. At first Rick didn't feel comfortable going but he finally agreed once I told him that Daniel's friend, Mary Canyon, was coming too. Rick is still married but he and his wife are separated. I wasn't interested in an intimate relationship with a married man, but I admit I was more than a little please that he seemed jealous of Daniel. I'd always found Rick physically attractive, even when I was utterly in love with Johnny. I reassured myself it was more likely Rick was just tired of hearing me talk about Daniel and the stories of the ancient Cahuilla Indians.

We'd hiked up from Lake Cahuilla, the reservoir that is part of a flood control project, to a small cove at the base of Torres Peak.

Each of us carried a pack loaded with goodies. Rick brought the wine. He surprised me by taking four crystal glasses cushioned with bubble wrap out of his backpack. Daniel's contribution to the feast was marinated salmons teaks packed in ice to keep them fresh. There was a stack of mesquite logs next to a fire pit in the cove. We rearranged the rocks into a circle small enough to fit the portable grill. Mary opened her pack, took out some small red potatoes, and coated them with fresh olive oil and fresh parsley. She wrapped each one carefully in aluminum foil and put them in the mesquite wood coals. Then, just before the fish steaks went on the grill, she wrapped some tender spears of asparagus with generous pats of butter in more foil and put the packet at the edge of the coals. I unpacked four ruby red glass dishes, my best silverware, and a hand-embroidered linen table cloth that I spread out on the sand. The meringue cookies made with dates and almonds that I'd baked the night before had miraculously survived.

"Mmmmm," I said between bites. "This is a great place for a picnic."

"Sure is!" Mary agreed, "But all this used to be under water here. Did you see the water line up there on the side of the mountain?"

"I wonder what caused that."

Mary turned to Daniel, "I know that the reservoir was named after a lake that used to be here, but how long ago was that?"

Daniel took a large sip of wine. "You're right. An ancient lake used to be here. It was formed from water from the Colorado River escaping and periodically covering most of the Imperial and Coachella Valleys, the last time about five hundred years ago. Most people called it Lake Cahuilla, named after my people who lived here then, but they called it by its Spanish name, *Agua Grande.* And now," he gestured toward Lake Cahuilla, "Just like the numbers of my people, it has grown smaller. Maybe we should call the reservoir *Agua Pequeña,* The Small Water."

Rick laughed, "Well, your *Agua Grande* almost happened again in 1905 when the Colorado River poured water into the Valley. Engineers finally got it stopped, but not before the Salton Sea was formed."

"Do you think it could happen again? I mean, could the desert be flooded up to the waterline again?"

"Sunny, just think about what a major earthquake here along the San Andreas Fault line could do," Daniel shook his head thoughtfully. "It's possible."

I grinned, "Yep, Mother Nature just shrugs and I'll be putting pontoons on the old trailer. Hey Rick, don't drink all of that by yourself. Share some around."

"You got it. Put your glasses over this way."

I raised my glass, "Here's to you, my good friends."

A full moon bathed the desert with light. Daniel put his arms around Mary and pulled her close. Rick had nothing to fear from Daniel. I've never seen him as happy as he was that evening. Mary had a contented smile on her face. They invited us to their wedding in September.

Daniel sang one of the bird songs in the Cahuilla language. He told us it was about the birds that sang at different times during the day. Mary laughed. She said that to the Cahuilla, it was like having a clock with feathers. Rick tapped me on the shoulder. "Sunshine, speaking of clocks, it's getting late. I have the early shift tomorrow."

Mary agreed. "Let's get this campsite cleaned up." She took Daniel's hand. "I think I need a moonlight hike after all that food. I want to fit into my wedding dress." Suddenly, marry smile disappeared and a tear flowed down her cheek.

Daniel noticed her change of mood. "Mary, what's wrong?"

"Nothing my love. I've chosen to be yours." She smiled lovingly at Daniel. "Forever."

Daniel wrapped his arms around Mary. "I felt it from the beginning."

"Yes, my love," Mary smiled enigmatically. Her golden-brown eyes scintillated in the moonlight. "From the beginning."

Daniel heard the intensity in her voice. "Mary?"

"Don't dwell on it, my love. Everything is as it should be."

Chapter 11

August 1998
Dry Springs Indian Reservation

Mary Canyon was in the backyard of her small brick home that had been built with funds from a government grant to the Dry Springs band of Cahuilla Indians before the casinos began to bring in money to the tribe. She heard the phone ringing and put down their basket of fresh-cut flowers, wiped her hands on her apron, and hurried through the back door. "Hello."

"Mary, I have to see you!"

"Michael Martinez! You have some nerve calling me."

"Mary, I know I blew it. I've lost everything that mattered to me … Lucy and my son. I need to talk to you. Please, don't refuse me. I have to explain about what happened. Daniel told me about the wedding."

"Michael, I'll see you. You better be sober or you will not be welcome in this house."

"I know what you heard, but I wasn't doing drugs. I swear. I was set up. I have to talk to you about Paulo."

"Okay, I'll be here."

"Thank you, Mary. I'm at the depot now. The bus is just loading. I should be there in about an hour. Thank you."

Mary put the phone down and went back to collect her basket of flowers. "Daniel would want me to try," she whispered to herself. "I'll do this for him." She put her gardening scissors down on the kitchen counter. "Now where did I put that vase?" Mary trimmed the excess leaves from the stems and left the flowers in the sink. Her dog was barking furiously. "Must be those damn coyotes sniffing around again."

She looked out the kitchen window but didn't see anything but mesquite trees and her car parked in the gravel driveway. The dog was quiet again and she went back to her cherished flowers, so difficult to grow in the alkaline soil on the Reservation.

The front door opened slowly and quietly. Mary was so absorbed in arranging the flowers that she didn't notice the man who stood behind her until it was too late. He picked up the scissors and stabbed her again and again. The pottery vase fell to the floor and broke. The flowers scattered in a colorful tangle as the spilled water commingled with her blood. She saw her attacker just before her eyes closed forever. "You?"

The man didn't have time to answer her. He had too much to accomplish before he left the house. He wiped his prints from the scissors and put them in the basket, then without expression, he took his knife from its sheath and carved the required loathsome design on the inside of the wooden door. He stood for a minute admiring his handiwork, replaced the knife, and stepped out into the late afternoon sun. He walked down the dirt road to where his truck was hidden. As he drove away he saw a young man walking toward Mary Canyon's house. *Perfect!* he grinned as he gunned the engine and yanked the steering wheel sharply to avoid hitting a mangy coyote running across the road.

"Mary? Mary, it's me, Michael." When no one answered, Michael Martinez walked around to the back of the house through the garden. He knocked on the back door and when there was no answer he turned the handle. It was open. He walked into the kitchen. He saw Mary's body and then his eyes were drawn unwillingly to the carving on the door. "Noooooooooooooo!" he screamed, spun around and ran frantically back the way he'd come. Fear outweighed reason. *Blood, so much blood. Have to get away! Nobody'll believe me. Gotta run...! Uhhh, that foul carving on the door. Daniel, oh brother please forgive me!*

Chapter 12

August 1998
Dry Springs Indian Reservation

Michael crashed blindly through clumps of mesquite and cats claw as though pursued by demons. The thorn-covered branches ripped his clothes. Blood oozed from deep scratches on his face and arms. Michael burst into the clearing where Daniel had built his adobe house. He pounded hopelessly on the door. "Oh, God please, please, Daniel, be home!" and sank to his knees sobbing. Dusk turned to night with no moon; the faraway sprinkle of stars in the Milky Way provided insignificant light on Earth.

The headlights from Daniel's truck illuminated his brother's huddled form. "What the …?" Daniel shuddered with alarm. "Michael?" Heart pounding, he raced to his brother and sheltered him in his arms.

"Daniel, oh God, Daniel, I'm sorry."

Daniel felt a sticky dampness and realized that Michael was covered with blood. "You're hurt! What happened?"

"No! You don't understand. It's Mary!"

Daniel staggered from an invisible gut wrenching blast. He was overcome by the bitter odor of dead flowers and in his mind's eye he saw Mary's figure shimmering just outside the corner of his vision. She was covered in blood, lying on the floor. Daniel opened his door and shoved Michael inside. "Stay here!" he ordered and raced off into the night. A coyote loped along behind the truck for a short distance and then squatted on his haunches, putting his thin muzzle in the air and howled.

A stranger to the reservation wouldn't easily follow the twisting dirt roads to Mary's house, but Daniel could drive them blindfolded. He skidded into Mary's driveway, saw the open door and dashed inside. A few minutes later two patrol cars, lights flashing, silently pulled in behind Daniel's truck.

The officers found Daniel rocking Mary's head in his arms. They quickly realized they'd walked in on a crime scene. One of the deputies grabbed Daniel and attempted to cuff him. Daniel swung angrily at the deputy, knocking him down. The other deputy quickly pulled Daniel's arms behind him and locked the handcuffs tight. Deputy Rick Tower reached down and placed his fingers on Mary's carotid artery. "No pulse, Smitty. She's dead," he stated matter-of-factly. "Mitch, call the wagon." Deputy Mitch Tolly swore, stood up and wiped his uniform with his hands, but the blood wouldn't brush off.

Daniel was struggling, hands behind his back. In the horror he saw the carving on Mary's door. He screamed, "Damn you, let me go! I didn't do this!"

Deputy Dwayne Smith gently pulled up on Daniel's handcuffed wrists, marched him out to the patrol car, protected his head and settled him into the rear seat. "Calm down Daniel. I saw the dust from your pick up. I know you didn't kill Mary, but you can't throw punches at the law. I promise you we'll find out who did this!"

Only Daniel saw the mountain lion spirit watching. "Iswatem!" he whispered in awe.

Chapter 13

July 09, 1999
Marietta Ranch

Big time training session this weekend. I took a deep breath, shrugged off the beginning of an impending depression, punched in Rick's number and got his answering machine. With a sigh I waited for the beep. "Rick, this weekend sounds good to me. I'll see you in the morning." I got my gear ready, packed a sandwich and an apple for lunch, filled two Evian bottles from the tap and put them in the freezer. Tomorrow the ice would melt slowly and the water would stay cold for many hours; a real treat when the temperature of a July day in the desert can soar to 120 degrees. I found my errant hat. Rick still teases me about the day I fainted and tumbled out of the saddle because I didn't wear a hat to protect me from the desert sun. Rick said I was lucky not to have heatstroke. He said my face was almost as red as the flowers on a hedgehog cactus. He accused me of being as prickly as one, too. I showered, turned on the oscillating fan, and fell asleep on top of the blue cotton bedspread.

I woke up to a mockingbird singing her morning repertoire of greetings to first light. It was a typical July dawn, deceptively cool. The weather report predicted the temperature would reach 110 degrees, and that's measured in the shade. The sky was clear. There was just a hint of breeze that, if it lasted, would make the afternoon heat bearable. The other two regular employees on the Marietta Ranch, Daniel Martinez and Leon MacIntyre, would take care of the place while I was gone. Leon's expertise is in training horses. He spent many afternoons working with Max, coaxing him to walk across water ditches and jump over mesquite branches. Max wasn't used to working in the desert. He'd been trained in the arena and on flat roads that made no demands on his horse sense. The trails up in the Whitewater area are rugged with boulders, heavy brush, and water-filled washes. The training that Leon gave Max has made him top horse in the qualifiers and is really going to come in handy tomorrow.

Leon and I hadn't started out as friends. I thought back to my first week on the job at the ranch. My dreams of working with horses had rapidly disappeared. I'd been hired to do the paperwork, order supplies, and pay the bills. I was just a bookkeeper with a fancy title. I felt sorry for myself and wondered why I ever decided to take the position. Frustrated, I'd turned off the computer. Carrie was staying with me for the weekend and we decided to ramble around the ranch. We'd just gone past the barn when Carrie and I heard a frantic mewing. There was a burrow under one of the outbuilding and we could just barely see the source of the sorrowful cries. There was no way I could get to the kittens. I left Carrie there and went looking for a shovel or some kind of tool that would help me get to them. I rushed into the tool shed and bumped into; I mean literally ran right into, and knocked down, a red-haired, red-faced leprechaun. The deeply etched furrows on his face increased the resemblance. He could have been forty or sixty; there was no way to know by looking.

"Who the hell are you?"

"My name is Sunny Morgan and I work here. Who are you?"

"I'm Leon MacIntyre, trainer on this ranch, and I've never heard of you!"

"Look, Leon MacIntyre, I don't have time to explain it to you right now. I heard some kittens crying and couldn't get to them. If you can help me, okay, but if not, get out of my way!"

"Jeez, lady."

He got up, brushing off the dust. "Where are these critters that are making you so unsociable? What do we need to rescue them?"

That was how I first met Leon. He never talked about his past. All I knew about him was that he was a bona-fide misanthrope with an Irish accent and a temper that flared up to match his hair. Carrie loved him at first sight. I watched them carry off the two kittens after Leon had buried the mother cat.

Later on, as I got to know Leon better, I learned that although he wouldn't tolerate any nonsense from people, he was always rescuing injured birds and other small critters. I think we were both surprised to discover an unexpected kinship.

I was still mourning Johnny then and I didn't have much fondness for human kind. I could appreciate that Leon didn't, either. I think he sensed that I was curled up inside my self like a hurt, wild animal.

Chapter 14

July 10, 1999
Marietta Ranch

I gave the trailer a quick once-over, put last night's dishes into the drainer, tossed the dirty laundry that had piled up for the last three days into the washing machine, and turned it on. If I was lucky I would get it into the dryer before Rick showed up. I gulped my coffee and wolfed down a piece of peanut butter toast, went out to the pasture and whistled for Max. He tossed his head, shook his mane, whinnied boisterously, and galloped full-speed toward me, kicking and bucking all the way. He knows when we're going on official business. Max thrives on the training sessions; it's like he was born to be a posse horse. Some of the horses barely meet the minimums of the qualification testing, but Max and I work as a team and have always qualified easily, even with sirens screaming, lights flashing, and firecrackers blasting.

At the last training, Max failed only one of twenty requirements. No matter how I coaxed him he refused to back up through the 'L' shaped obstacle, 36" wide and 10' long on each side, but none of the other horses would do it either. I was going to have to set up an 'L' for practice. At the end of the qualification we still had the highest score. Not even Blackfoot, Rick's fox-trotter, did better. Posse horses have to prove they can perform under difficult conditions so they don't endanger the public we serve. If our horses don't qualify at the training, we don't go on call-outs.

Rick drove up in the midst of billowing dust, jumped out of the truck, and helped me get my gear loaded. Max and I have had some serious disagreements about his travel arrangements, but when I opened the back door of the horse trailer, to my amazement he walked right in to take his place beside Blackfoot.

Rick was in a hurry. I was just latching the trailer door when he hollered, "Hey Sunshine, let's go! Couldn't ask for a more beautiful morning." I bounced into the cab. Rick had the truck moving toward the gate before I could get my seatbelt fastened.

"Thanks for waiting for me, Rick. For a second there I thought you guys were leaving without me. What's the scenario for our team today?"

"I don't know, but Brad promised it was going to be good."

Sergeant Brad Johnson is the deputy in charge of Desert Posse events and training. He's forty-eight, has a little balding spot which he usually covers with a Stetson hat, and a broken heart that he can't hide. His ex-wife Marilyn doesn't ride; she's afraid of horses and was jealous of the time Brad spent with the posse. I couldn't blame her. When Brad wasn't on duty he was working on posse business. Marilyn finally gave him an ultimatum: "It's me or the posse." He tried to spend more time with her but he couldn't give up the posse. In the end she couldn't take it.

Rick looked at me with concern on his face. "You remember that disc you found when we recovered Lucy Martinez's remains? We ran it through our lab. It had some financial records on it, but most of the data was ruined by the weather."

"Aren't there ways to recover the data?"

"I wondered about that, too. The Feds have the disc now."

"Isn't it unusual for the Feds to get involved in something like this?"

"I don't second-guess the brass."

"I really hoped there would be something."

"Yeah, but there's no way it could still be intact after being out there that long. Too bad, but we have other fish to fry today."

"Rick, you don't think …?"

He cut me off. "Anything you need to get on the way? We have about an hour drive up to the Whitewater cutoff. I want to get to Patty's place before someone else gets my spot under the cottonwood tree."

Damn. I'd hoped that disc would give us some answers. But Rick was right; we did have other things to do today.

I expected to hear about the case Rick was working on but he was unusually quiet. Sometimes he shuts down; just sits there without saying a word like he's a million miles away, but he's never moody when he's teaching. I enrolled in his firearms course; mandatory if I wanted to carry a gun. I couldn't wait to shoot the Glock pistol that I'd just purchased.

Rick showed me how to hold the gun in firing position and then surprised me when he put a dime on the front sight. "Sunshine, keep your sight on the money and the money on the sight."

He wouldn't even let me load my gun until I'd practiced for hours with my arm extended and that damn ten cent piece balanced on the front sight until I'd developed the balance and strength necessary to control my shots. I finished the course shooting a 245, a better than average score.

We were heading out for a glorious adventure, but Rick didn't seem to be his usual self. "Rick, is anything wrong?"

"No, I'm just tired. Had to pull a double shift. Sorry I'm such bad company." Okay, so he didn't feel like talking right then. He'd get over it.

We drove west on I-10 with San Jacinto Peak over ten thousand feet high on the left and Mt. San Gorgonio towering like a mighty twin on the right. Rick's truck has air conditioning, which is the only comfortable way to travel through the desert. The early morning sky was a smorgasbord of color; tasty oranges and radiant pinks. Going up the interstate toward the San Gorgonio Pass, the view is interrupted by an army of wind turbine generators.

"Rick, check out those wind machines. Just think, some day enough energy could be harvested from those rotating propellers to supply electricity to every home in the valley."

"Sunny, don't go blind looking at the bright side. It'll never happen. What you see there is a tax write-off for some millionaire."

"It's not a scam. They really do generate electricity."

"Yeah, but don't expect us to see the benefits of it anytime soon. Tourists aren't the only ones who complain about the towers spoiling their view. Don't forget, it's ecologists who are filing lawsuits to protect the sand dune habitat of your endangered fringe-toed lizard."

"Just the same, production of wind energy is less harmful to the environment than the burning of fossil fuels. It's worth a try."

"Sunny, you want to believe that, okay. I'll believe it when I see the results."

"Maybe you're right but you know there's a chance."

"Besides, the wind towers are ugly! They ruin the view."

I shook my head insistently. "Rick, those whirling blades have always made me think of giant gymnasts somersaulting in the wind."

"Great image for poetry Sunny, but they really annoy me. I like to see the scenery without the machinery. See, I can spout poetry, too. Hey, you don't have to flash those green eyes of yours at me."

I turned away and stared out the window.

As the truck pulled the horse trailer easily up the Whitewater grade, Rick broke the silence. "You know, there was a missing person report filed last week; a twelve year old girl. She was out here visiting her father for the summer. He reported her missing when she didn't come home for a Fourth of July party at a friend's house just a couple of blocks away. When she wasn't home in time for dinner, he called the house. They said the party was over at four o'clock. Apparently the girl, Lindy Dibbs, left before the party was over. According to the other kids she was in a bad mood."

"Did anyone see her after the party?"

"No, at least we haven't had any witness come forward. She wore jeans, a white tee-shirt with Garfield on the front, and white tennis shoes. When she left, she had on a gold hat with bright blue streamers, you know, those party favors that kids get. You'd think someone would at least remember the hat, but we talked to the kids at the party, canvassed the neighborhood, showed her photo to the local bus drivers and the employees at the bus depot, even talked with the cabbies. Nobody saw her."

"Another sad face for the milk cartons. When I worked at the shelter we saw kids with cigarette burns and broken arms, their backs scarred from beatings. The abusers always blame the kids and the kids always blame themselves. There was only one girl who got picked up by some slime-ball and ended up doing drugs and hooking. She was only thirteen."

Rick shook his head grimly. "I know."

"What do you think happened to the Dibbs girl? Do you think she could have been abducted?" I shivered. "Remember what you and Smitty were saying about a serial killer."

"I don't know, to be honest with you, but there were some problems between the girl and her stepmother. The girl refused to help with some housework and the stepmother grounded her. She went to her dad and complained Said she wanted to go back home to L.A because her stepmother hated her. It was her summer vacation and she didn't want to spend it mopping floors. Her dad felt guilty and let her go to the party. His wife discovered about fifty dollars missing from her purse. I figure the girl will turn up at her mother's in Los Angeles. Apparently this is not the first time she's run away."

"That's sad. Too many children run away from home and are never seen again. I talked to Deputy Jan Worthman yesterday. She gave me some statistics on the number of runaways here in the desert. It's scary. She started the program where deputies and volunteers go to the schools and talk with the kids about the dangers out there, what do to if they are approached, and where to go for help."

Rick seemed relieved to have changed the subject. "Yeah, and it works, too. Last month we got a report that a guy was trying to get a couple of middle school girls into his car. They screamed, ran away, and told the crossing guard. The guy took off like a shot, but the girls gave us a description of him, the car, and a license plate number. Got him in a couple of hours. Jan gave a presentation to the kids at that school just the week before."

"That's great."

"Yep."

"Rick, I've been meaning to ask you about something. I've been getting the weirdest calls. I answer the phone and nobody says anything. I know someone is there because I can hear breathing. It's been happening for a while now. I didn't think much about it at first because it didn't happen very often, maybe once every couple of months. I assumed it was just a prank. But recently it's been happening a lot. What scares me is that the calls have changes. At first I just heard breathing and the person hung up. Last week I was about to hang up when I heard a voice, just a gruff voice, that said, 'Sunny.' That was all."

"Did you report the call?"

:Yeah, and I called the phone company. They suggested that I changed my phone number. Rick, I already have an unlisted number and I hate to change it, but maybe I should."

"Sounds like a good idea. You ought to get caller ID for your phone, too. There's a chance you could find out who's doing it. You get the number, and I'll trace the guy."

"Thanks. We'll nail the creep next time. I almost hope he does call again." I didn't tell Rick that I'd already had the phone company put caller ID on my phone. He's a good friend, but as much as I appreciate his advice, I could take care of myself. The next time I got a call from that cowardly creep, his ass was mine.

Chapter 15

July 1999
Shaggy Pines Ranch

Handy, a heavy-set, sour-faced man in his thirties, had driven about a half-mile north of Pinyon Pine Restaurant and turned right, bumping too fast over a cattle guard. He drove more slowly down the washed out dirt road through a small forest of pinyon pines to the farmhouse where Tobias and Earl were waiting next to an old barn built with rough lumber. Aluminum doors lay abandoned against the side of the structure. The barn had probably sheltered sheep or cattle at one time. Now the roof was partially gone and there was nothing but weeds, beer cans, and broken bottles around the place. Inside the barn, almost out of sight, was Earl's pickup truck.

Tobias had long, straggly, dishwater-blonde hair and a beard with leftovers from breakfast still smeared in it. He wasn't wearing a shirt and his overalls looked like they'd never been washed. Earl was thinner and taller than Tobias, his black mustache drooped down a narrow, pinched face. He wore a clean plaid flannel shirt, jeans, and well-worn hiking boots. He held a shotgun angled toward the road. Neither of the men smiled when they saw the green station wagon drive in. Earl lowered the gun the rest of the way.

Handy growled, "Come on; help me get the supplies in the barn. A highway patrol car followed me part way up the hill. When his lights started flashing, I was sure I was busted. Lucky for him he pulled around me and kept on going. Earl, grab the tarp off those barrels. Move it. We have to cook up a new batch. I've got a buyer in L.A. who wants his shipment of meth yesterday."

"Okay," Earl grumbled, leaning the gun against the car, "Don't put your balls in a blender. We're all set to go except for the solvent."

Earl grabbed a barrel and rolled it into the barn. As Tobias pushed the other barrel inside, he kicked at a mangy German

Shepherd puppy. The pup limped on three legs and slunk out of reach. He growled at Tobias from a safe spot behind the truck.

"Earl, if you don't keep that mutt out of my way I'm going to shoot her. Always digging. Always shitting where I walk. No account watchdog. Yeah, she'd sit there with her tongue hanging out and watch while the cops walk right in."

"You just worry about getting this shipment put together. Leave the dog alone. She's cleaner than you are, Toby. Has better manners, too."

"Aw, Handy, you got no call to bad-mouth me. I do my job. I just can't stand to see that sorry excuse for a dog hanging around all the time. Should'a put her out of her misery when she got her leg caught in my coyote trap."

"You're lucky you didn't step in your own damn trap."

Chapter 16

July 10, 1999

Rick pointed to the right, "There's the turnoff to Whitewater. Patty Kimball's ranch is only a mile or so."

At our June posse meeting, Patty, a reserve deputy and posse member had offered her ranch for the exercise. We would camp overnight at her place because there weren't any public facilities near that stretch of the Pacific Crest Trail. I was already anticipating sitting around the campfire and listening to Patty play old cowboy songs on her guitar. She and Johnny used to play a mean duet, but I'm not going to live in the past this weekend. Music and song would make me forget my saddle-sore muscles and maybe this time I wouldn't think about Johnny. The pancake breakfast the morning after the training exercise is not for the diet-conscious. I could almost taste the toppings and syrups including my favorite, choke cherry preserves. There'd be sausage, bacon, and a huge plate of watermelon, casaba, honeydew, kiwi, with fresh pineapple slices to boot. I gained five pounds just thinking about it.

Rick parked the truck next to an ancient cottonwood; its broad open crown already cast an inviting shade, even this early in the morning. The only rig there besides Patty's belonged to Jim Moore, a volunteer posse member.

I looked down the road we had just drive over and saw more dust rising. "Here comes the posse!" I glanced back at Rick.

He gave me a broad smile. "Yep." He'd already claimed his favorite spot.

The next half hour was spent getting organized. The horses were already saddled and the gear checked when Brad Johnson, who was in charge of the briefing, handed out the scenario sheets. Each team had a different mission. Rick was our team leader. He carried the radio for communication with the Command Post.

Our team's instructions required us to ride as far as Red Dome, an unusual rock formation close to the beginning of the Mission Creek trail. There's not another cluster of rocks of the same color in the area. It looks like a large, rounded, red-brown breast protruding from a wash covered with glistening white rocks.

Our training objective was to find a thirty-nine year-old male with diabetes who had been hiking alone up the Mission Creek Trail. According to the scenario he was eight hours overdue and his wife had reported him missing. We were to scout the area around Red Dome and, if we found the hiker, assess the situation and provide first aid. We weren't told when the man had his last insulin injection or if he carried any with him. Each of us carried a "low pack" in case he had an insulin reaction. An immediate dose of glucose-rich food followed by a protein and carbohydrate helps if the victim is conscious; but with the information given in this scenario, it was more likely our victim would be in trouble from exposure, dehydration, and exhaustion compounded by his medical condition. In a real search, finding the victim quickly would make the difference between life and death.

There were four of us on our team and we were the first to head out. Patty Kimball and Jeff Newhowser, both riding quarter horses, were behind Rick and me. Rick told me that Jeff was a tough boss and demanded absolute loyalty and excellence form his officers. He'd just joined the posse as a volunteer recently, still felt a little uncomfortable on a horse, but he was determined to learn. Jan Worthman told me why. Jeff's wife had been camping with his three daughters when a forest fire had rushed through the area where they were. A mountain search and rescue team found them safe; sheltered in a cave. I understand why Jeff wants to help other families who feel that same fear of losing their loved ones. Payback isn't always negative.

The morning was beginning to warm up and a slight breeze blew a few errant clouds across the iridescent blue sky. We'd ridden about half a mile when I spotted a small camper's shovel; the kind that folds up for easy packing. It was lying just off the side of the road. "Rick, look over there. Maybe that's where our missing hiker went off the road."

Rick got on the radio and reported what we'd found. Brad radioed back that the hiker had only taken a day-pack; no shovel.

"Sunshine," Rick smiled at me. "Good going! The shovel isn't part of our scenario; probably fell of a camper's vehicle. We do treat our training searches just like a real search and call in when we find anything that might help us. Command Post tells us whether to flag it or not."

Rick turned in the saddle and shouted, "Hey Patty is Smitty going to be at the barbecue?"

"He said he'd try to be back in time to help out, but for sure he'll be there to eat." Patty laughed.

Max and Blackfoot eased into the gait their breed is famous for. Patty and Jeff didn't look quite as comfortable on their quarter horses, but were holding their own. Soon, the four of us rode off the road and were on the trailhead to Red Dome. The trail was in bad condition and the horses had to pick their way carefully over the rocks. There isn't much wildlife visible during the daylight hours in summer, but we startled a black-tailed jackrabbit poised for flight; his long ears briefly pointed in our direction before he fled into the desert brush.

After about half an hour, we took a short break near a desert willow tree to rest the horses and check their hooves for stones. Patty used her hoof pick to pry a small stone from Red's right front hoof. He thanked her by butting her with his head and almost knocking her over. Max was taking advantage of the break. He had is head down and his eyes were almost closed. I was about to grab the reins when I saw a rattlesnake at least three feet long sliding out of the brush toward us. I knew enough about rattlers to freeze. I nearly panicked as the snake went between Max's legs and on down the bank of the wash. Miraculously Max didn't even notice. It was a breath-holding moment, but after a few erratic heartbeats I managed to remount. The snake had no interest in us, and as long as we didn't threaten him he was content to go on his way. I quieted my breathing. "Go on your way, little brother," I whispered. Daniel had told me the story about Mukat, the Creator, who had given Rattlesnake two cactus thorns for teeth and poison to protect him from those who tormented him. Rattlesnake had delivered the first death in the world.

Rick chuckled at my distress. "Sunshine, you and Max are too tough to make a good breakfast," Rick chortled. "That snake probably already swallowed a tender filet of kangaroo rat." Rick swung into the saddle and led the way up the trail.

"Rick, if that rattler had gone under Blackfoot you wouldn't make any jokes."

"Lighten up, Sunshine."

Jeff turned to Rick, "That was pretty scary. What if her horse had spotted that diamondback?"

Patty laughed. "Well, he didn't, did he? What doesn't happen doesn't hurt."

I gritted my teeth, "Thanks a lot Patty. You enjoy the excitement?"

"No Sunny. Can't say that I did. You were lucky. Keep your eyes open. We may just find some clues around here. Too bad we didn't ask the snake for directions."

Jeff leaned over to Patty and said, "Cut it out Patty. Keep your eyes on the trail. You keep teasing Sunny and you could miss something."

Patty got a serious look on her face. "Jeff, I don't miss nothing! I may be joking around now, but a real search is different, you'll see. This is just an exercise."

"Sorry Patty. Didn't mean to question your competence."

Rick put an end to the debate. "Let's get going. We have a hiker to find." He could have gotten heavy with Patty but he let it go this time. He never thinks of our training as 'just an exercise'.

It was getting hot and I was beginning to sweat under my hat. I took a long drink from one of my water bottles. I didn't want to get dehydrated. There was still some ice in the bottle. I put the container against the back of my neck. It felt good! We rode for another half-hour before we came up out of the wash and saw Red Dome in the distance. Rick signaled for us to stop. He pointed down at the trail.

"See that? Those boot prints have the same circle in the middle as the drawing we got from Brad. Check out those tracks. He's not walking very straight; the tracks are all over the place. Looks like we've found our guy and he's in trouble."

He radioed Command Post. "CP, this is Team One. We've found the hiker's boot prints. Request further instructions."

"This is Command Post. Flag and proceed."

"Ten-four"

Rick took out a roll of orange flagging tape, attached it to an ice cream stick with a clothespin, and stuck it in the sand where the prints started.

Careful not to let the horses step on the boot prints, we followed the tracks for a while and then lost them on rocky ground.

Patty called out, "There's a canteen over there beside the trail." I dismounted, picked it up, and shook it. "Empty."

"Maybe this is where he left the trail." I was getting into the excitement of the search.

"Could be, Sunshine. Any more tracks?"

"Over here!" Jeff was excited. "I found them!" He pointed to the right of the trail. "Keep the horses back! The guy's really stumbling around. I think he fell down there. See the depression in the sand? Look! There's his daypack."

Rick led Blackfoot over to where Jeff was pointing. "Yeah, I think you're right. Be careful. We don't want to lose him."

The rest of our team dismounted. We led the horses off the trail and down the wash. The terrain was hard to negotiate because we had to avoid some large boulders. The brush and salt cedars were so thick we couldn't see too far ahead. We'd split up and walked about a hundred yards more when Max snorted and tossed his head. He shied away from a large boulder. I settled him down. The missing hiker was crumpled up beside the rock where he'd tried to find shade.

We knew at once he was our hiker because the poster board sign on his back said, "VICTIM". Rick handed the radio to me and I immediately radioed our position to CP and requested a 'medi-vac' helicopter. "We found the hiker. He appears to be unconscious."

Jeff shook the victim a lot harder than necessary. "Are you all right? Can you hear me?" There was no response.

Patty checked for breathing and injuries. The victim was not only breathing, he was trying not to laugh.

Word from Command Post was, "Good work! Tell Jim he did a great job setting up this exercise. Come on home."

Jim Moore got up, brushed himself off, and retrieved his horse from behind the dense brush. We got back on our horses laughing as Jim tried to hold his horse and shake sand out of his boots at the same time. Jim is just shy of forty; six feet of tanned, well-muscled cowboy. He shoes horses for a living and rides with the posse for pleasure. His cockeyed grin and brown bedroom eyes would make a stone statue melt. If he weren't very married I'd think seriously about throwing my lasso around that one. Rick told me there have been a few women on the posse who've tried. Try is as far as they got.

"I was sure I was going to die of heatstroke 'fore you guys found me."

"Uh huh, Jim." Patty smirked, "We should have left you here for the coyotes."

The way Patty said it made me wonder if she'd been one of the women who had tried.

With that crazy lopsided grin, Jim replied, "Hey, it's hard work getting lost. Do you know how early I had to get up this morning just so you dudes could make points? If I hadn't invited the Mrs. along you wouldn't have had a victim to find. She would have had me hogtied and branded back at the ranch."

We started back down the trail in good spirits knowing that our successful search would be rewarded with a mouth-watering barbecue that night. Mission accomplished! We were already back on Whitewater Canyon Road when Patty and I needed a pit-stop. Sometimes being a woman is an inconvenience. The guys held our horses and we went down the gravelly bank toward some thick brush.

Patty nearly tripped over a dead branch. My boots made crunching sounds in the wash as I walked toward the bushes.

There was the unmistakable odor of a dead animal somewhere nearby. A glint of gold caught my eye. I looked closer. It was a small gold hat with a single blue streamer tangled in a bush. I felt chilled and tried to ignore the high-pitched whine in my head.

"Rick!" I yelled, "My God, it's her hat!" I knew it had to belong to Lindy Dibbs, the missing girl, and by the unmistakable reek of death, I knew her body was nearby. I could see the shape of a small, white tennis shoe under the branches.

Patty was right behind me. "Sunny, what's going on?"

I was shaking with dread. I knew if I didn't pull myself together Rick would ship me home. Even with the horror of what I was sure we'd find I wanted to be a part of this one. "Patty," I managed to choke out, "Lindy Dibbs, she was wearing a hat like that when she disappeared." I pointed toward the bush.

Rick came scrambling down the side of the wash. "Sunny, what the hell?" Then he saw the blue streamer snaking in the breeze and the little gold hat stuck in the bush. He knew.

"Don't go any closer. Sunny, Patty, get back over here!" All of a sudden he was totally professional. "Don't destroy any evidence."

Rick got on the radio. "We have a situation here."

He requested a confidential channel and gave Brad our location. "Call Mitch. He's working homicide detail this weekend. I think we may have found the Dibbs girl." Brad told us to stay put and wait for mobile units.

Patty and I tramped across the road. We relieved ourselves and went back to the horses.

I leaned up against Max's sweaty neck. The salty horse lather helped to soften the smell of death that seemed to stick inside my nose. The five of us waited silently by the side of the road.

It seemed to take forever before the back and whites arrived with the homicide detectives. They cordoned off the area with yellow crime scene tape. Ernie Wood drove up in the newly purchased mobile forensic lab. Smiling, he stepped out of the converted motor home like he was on vacation. The detectives debriefed us one at a time.

Since I had found her, I was first. Mitch questioned, "Sunny, how'd you find the body?"

"I needed to pee. Patty and I went down the side of the wash to find a good bush. I saw a flash of gold and then the blue ribbon. Rick told me about the missing girl on the drive up to Patty's ranch. He made a point about the hat she was wearing when she disappeared, but Mitch, it was the smell."

Mitch nodded, "Once you've smelled death you don't ever forget it. Now I want you to think back. Did you see any tire tracks or footprints near the body?"

"No, there were only coyote tracks. I didn't see any tire tracks or signs that people had been there recently; just the hat and the smell. Wait a minute. Where I went down the embankment I remember Patty tripped over a branch that looked like it had been ripped off one of the bushes."

"We found it. The killer probably used it to brush out his tracks. Was there anything unusual that you remember seeing on Whitewater Canyon Road or on the trail?"

I remembered the shovel I found beside the road. "Mitch, I don't know if it's important, but about a mile up the road from Patty's place close to where the trail to Red Dome takes off, we did find a small folding shovel, you know the kind a hiker would pack. I thought it might belong to the missing hiker scenario, but it didn't."

"Do you think you could find it again?"

"It was right by the road. I think I could see it from a car if we drove slowly."

"Let's go check it out." Mitch headed for his patrol car.

We drove back down the road and when we got close to where I saw the shovel I asked him to slow down. I missed it on the first drive by, but on the way back I spotted it still lying off the side of the road. "There it is!"

Mitch got out of the unit and walked over to the shovel. He bent down to look at it. "Did you guys pick it up?"

"No, we radioed CP and Brad told us to go on."

"That's good because it looks like there's blood on the handle."

Mitch radioed Ernie that more evidence had been found. After Ernie arrived, Mitch and I went back to the scene.

"What now?"

"Sunny we're going to do our best to get the perp who did this. You've helped us get a step closer."

"Yeah Mitch. I joined the posse to save people, not to find dead children."

"You don't always have a happily ever after in this job. You know that." Mitch put both hands on my shoulders. "Johnny was a good friend of mine. I miss him too."

Tears began to form in my eyes, but I didn't cry. I wouldn't let Mitch see that he had reached a very private grief. It belonged to me.

I shook off the emotion and Mitch's hands. I glanced stubbornly around his broad shoulders. The body had been recovered. Two deputies held the orange molded plastic stretcher waiting to load the body into the coroner's van. Just before they zipped up the body bag I walked over to the stretcher and saw what that butcher had done to Lindy Dibbs.

Patty, Jeff, and Jim were already on their horses. Rick held Blackfoot and Max. "Let's go Sunshine. There's nothing else we can do here." Rick and I got on our horses and caught up with the rest of our team. We rode by the spot where Ernie was taking pictures of the site where we had found the shovel. I could see by the black powder on the handle that he'd already dusted it for fingerprints.

Ernie looked up at us and grinned malevolently. He picked up the shovel with his gloved hands and waved it at us. Max spooked and I grabbed onto the saddle horn and reined him in away from Ernie.

I felt like I was about to vomit. I didn't appreciate Ernie's macabre sense of humor. He may know his job, but he doesn't know horses.

Rick rode Blackfoot right next to Ernie and I guess he must have read him the riot act because Ernie looked chagrined. He came over to apologize for scaring my horse. Rick must have noticed that I was turning green, but he didn't look so good himself after the little girl's body was recovered.

"Sunshine, come on. Let's get back to Patty's. That's just Ernie's way. When you see as much death as Ernie does, you have to develop some kind of defense or you wouldn't sleep nights."

I knew Rick was right, but it still seemed callused. That poor little girl. The terror she must have endured was just beginning to hit me.

Chapter 17

July 10, 1999

Only the sound of the horses' hooves crunching on the gravel could be heard as we silently rode up the road to Patty's ranch. An aura of gloom had descended on our team. I dismounted and led Max into one of the corrals, unsaddled, and rubbed him down. The familiar routine kept me calm; at least on the outside. I'd seen living children with unimaginable injuries, but nothing could have prepared me for the mutilated body of a little girl partially buried; the streamer from her party hat waiving like a flag beside her.

Brad was waiting for us on the ranch house porch. He'd already assembled the other posse members and reported to the other teams our discovery of the Dibbs girl's body. "The Sheriff's Department has officially asked for our assistance in the Dibbs murder case. Tomorrow morning we'll be doing an evidence search. We'll leave the horses here, drive to the scene, and do a line search in the area around where the girl's body was found. For now we might as well set up camp. First thing tomorrow we'll plan the search, but for now take a break and set up your campsites. We've all had a rough day and we're going to have a long day tomorrow."

There would be no fancy breakfast in the morning. This was the real thing, not an exercise.

"Sunshine, you okay?" Rick whispered as we unloaded the truck. "That was a helluva shock."

No, I'm not okay, I thought to myself. "Yep. I'll live." I wasn't going to let anybody know how disturbed I was, especially Rick. After Max was fed and watered, I went into the kitchen to help Patty cut up the chickens while she made her special barbecue sauce. I hadn't eaten lunch, but I wasn't hungry. I tried not to think about Lindy Dibbs as I was slicing and chopping the chicken carcasses.

Brad used a chain saw to cut the mesquite limbs into two foot lengths, and Rick wielded the sledge hammer and wedges to split them into chunks for the barbecue; a fifty gallon drum cut in half and welded on a stand with the top half of the drum attached with hinges to make a cover. The larger logs went into the fire pit. Jim scrubbed the large iron grate with a wire brush. Jan Worthman set up chairs around the fire pit. Grace Cotton and her husband Allen, a retired deputy, squeezed Valencia oranges, the last fruit of the season on the trees from their citrus ranch. They always kept some in cold storage for our July training. Allen's margaritas are famous. He says you have to use fresh squeezed fruit to get a deep orange color and with a little salt and a slice of lime you don't even have to add tequila. Everyone was busy with something, but we were all a lot quieter than usual.

The sun was casting long shadows when the smell of mesquite smoke filled the air. It would be about an hour before we put the chicken on to cook. Mesquite burns hot and chicken requires slow cooking. We would have to wait for the coals to be just right. We were just about to put the chicken on the barbecue when Smitty, the only black deputy on the force, cruised up in his 1057 red Corvette. He and Patty had been sharing life and love for the last six months. They were waiting for Patty's divorce to become final so they could tie the knot.

"Hey, Smitty!" Rick waved. "You got here just in time. The hard work is all done."

"Yep, I know how to plan. I just got off shift. I heard on the radio that you found the Dibbs girl's body. I went up to the scene to see if I could help out, but they were ready to leave. Body's gone," Smitty reported, "but Ernie's still taking his grisly pictures. Even he said it was ugly."

Rick wasn't smiling. "Yep, ugly doesn't even begin to describe it."

Smitty paused uncertainly, "I guess you guys will be doing the evidence search in the morning." He regained his composure. "I'm off tomorrow. I'd like to go with you."

Rick extended both his hands and gripped Smitty's. "Come on, we need all the help we can get."

Patty came out of the house wiping her hands on a towel. She put her arms around Smitty and kissed him lightly on the cheek. "I'm glad you could get off your shift early. It's been a rough day."

Rick watched Smitty give Patty a deep kiss. "Hey, if it's not too much to ask, turn loose of Patty for just a few minutes and give us a hand with the chicken. You've got to earn your keep around here somehow."

Smitty blustered, "Right, just give me the tongs and I'll show you how it's done."

We all gathered around the barbecue grill to watch the first pieces go on and then sat down in the chairs by the fire pit. Rick lit the fire just as the sun disappeared; a hint of orange caressing the clouds that concealed San Jacinto Peak.

The kindling blazed high and started the logs burning. Looking into the flames and listening to the crackle of the campfire relaxed the tension in my neck and shoulders. My nausea gone, I began to look forward to an evening with friends.

Allen made margaritas for all of us. "With or without?" he asked.

There was a chorus of 'With!' Only Allen chose to have his without. He's been on the wagon for three years now.

After we finished the last of the barbecue chicken, buttered corn on the cob, cheese-filled rolls, and potato salad, and there were only a few crumbs left from the upside-down pineapple cake, Patty brought out her guitar and began to sing *Little Joe the Wrangler*; a sad song about a young boy who joined a cattle drive and was killed during a stampede. It seemed like a singularly bad choice of songs in light of the day's events. The only one that could have been worse in my estimation was *You Are My Sunshine*.

Smitty broke the mood, "Patty, come on, you're breaking my heart. Play *Finnegan's Wake*. At least that song has a few laughs."

"Okay my love, you asked for it!"

Patty played and sang it and a few more rollicking Irish songs and then, in a cheerful mood that still seemed a little forced, everyone pitched in to clean up. Too soon it was time to say good night. We'd shared a pleasant evening, but underlying the singing and laughter was the knowledge that there was a monstrous child killer out there. I felt safe with half the posse camped all around me, but thinking about Lindy Dibbs left me in a somber mood.

Some of the posse members had campers, but Rick and I got our sleeping bags and put them out under the night sky. "See you in the morning, Sunshine."

"Good night, Rick." I crawled into my bag, blessing the self-inflatable air mattress that I purchased last summer after spending too many nights tossing and turning on ricks and gravel. With it under my tired bones, I drifted into sleep.

"Sunshine, you are so beautiful." He began to unweave my braids. "I want to look into the dark pools of your green eyes and lose myself in the ripples of your long raven hair. We will be together forever." With one finger he slowly traced a line from my nipple down; lightly circled my stomach sending chills of pleasure through me. He turned my face toward his and kissed me, lightly touching my lips with his tongue and then more deeply. When he sensed that I couldn't wait any longer he eased my legs open with his, and gently guided himself between my thighs. I was so wet; so ready. He was hard and eager. I felt him slowly move inside me. The shot exploded. There was blood everywhere; hot blood dripping down my naked body.

I screamed, "No! Johnny!"

I could still smell the sweet, over-ripe odor of blood when Rick shook me awake. "Sunshine", he said quietly, "It's okay Sunshine. You're okay."

Then the tears came. No sound, just tears rolling across my cheeks into my ears. I opened my eyes and saw the blurry stars above and heard an owl in the cottonwood tree, softly hooting to his mate. It was that dream again, the same damn dream. It never starts the same way, but the end is always the same. Johnny is dead. The tears flowed in earnest. I crawled out of the sleeping back and went to the truck to get some tissues. Rick started to follow me and then turned around and let me go.

The next morning Smitty left his Corvette at the ranch and drove Patty's four-wheel drive Dodge. Rick unhitched the horse trailer from the Chevy and we all drove up Whitewater Canyon Road to the wash where I'd discovered the body. Brad told us to walk in a horizontal line about fifteen feet apart so that we could check the area on both sides and not miss something in a blind spot. I found some spent shotgun shells, a few rusty cans, a horseshoe with the nails still in the holes, but nothing else.

We did three more sweeps before Brad called a halt to the search. Hot and sweaty, we were on our way back passing close to the crime scene, when Jeff called out. He'd found a round silver pendant about one and a half inches in diameter, with a picture of a frog or a toad engraved on one side, and some zigzag designs on the other. The silver chain was broken. We called it in and flagged it, then we looked more closely around the area, but we didn't find anything else. The charm might have nothing to do with the murder but because of its proximity to the body, I was sure it had something to do with Lindy Dibbs' murder.

Chapter 18

August 8, 1999
Marietta Ranch

I'd survived the July heat, but in August survival is less sure. The fetid odor of millions of dead fish blows in from the dying Salton Sea and the unrelenting humidity of a monsoon weather pattern creates a noxious environment. Life in the low desert becomes unbearable if you don't have air conditioning. My ancient swamp cooler rattled on, adding moisture to the already sodden air. I was too miserable to sleep so I opened the front door of my sweat lodge on wheels and watched sheet lightning flash over the high desert hills. It was cooler outside the trailer and, except for the rumble of thunder and an occasional semi speeding down 'killer' Highway 86, the night was quiet.

I heard the helicopter coming from the direction of our local airport. It circled overhead and spewed a wide bright streak of light through the long rows of date trees at the end of the ranch. The search light swept down the road past my trailer and back to the highway again. Sirens whined in the distance.

My phone rang. I got inside before the answering machine picked up and grabbed the phone, knocking it off the table. I finally got the receiver to my ear. It was Rick. "Sunshine, what happened?" He sounded anxious.

"Nothing, I just dropped the phone."

"I'm glad you're still awake."

"Who could sleep on a night like this?" Rick teases me that I better get an air conditioner in my bedroom or I'll never get a guy to spend the night. He may be right. Maybe that's why I don't. After Johnny was killed I gained 30 pounds, stopped wearing makeup, gave my suits and high heels to Goodwill, and threw away my nylons. When I joined the local posse as a volunteer, I lost the weight but chose to spend time with my horse searching for lost hikers and riding the perimeters at celebrity golf tournaments instead of looking for relationships. I still like my horse better than people. If it weren't for the camaraderie and support of the posse members, I probably would have become a hermit. And then there is Daniel, my mentor and friend.

There was an overtone of genuine concern in Rick's voice, "Sunshine, the reason I called; there's a bad actor down your way. CHP pulled over a pickup truck for a broken tail light just about half a mile from your place. We've got an officer down. The driver bailed and started shooting. He took off down the date grove. Be careful, okay? I worry about you being alone over there."

My employers' travel the horse-show circuit and rarely spend much time on their desert ranch; none at all in the summer. At night I'm the only two-legged being who sleeps on the ranch in August.

"This guy is dangerous. Watch out for yourself. We've got a chopper out, but no luck so far. I'm heading out now."

"Thanks for calling. I saw the helicopter search light from my porch. I wondered what was going on."

"If it's all right with you, I'll be over around noontime tomorrow. I want to check out Max's hind foot. I noticed he was a little tender the last time we went riding."

I knew he was coming over to check on me, but for once I didn't let Rick's protectiveness bother me. "See you tomorrow. I'm glad I don't have to chase the bad guys tonight. This humidity is a killer!"

I hung up the phone and checked the door. I opened the lock box where I keep my Glock Model 22-40 caliber semi-automatic pistol. I carefully grasped the gun, racked the slide, and put it on the bedside table. Rick calls it my Tupperware gun because it has a plastic grip and part of the frame is plastic, too. I like it because it's light, yet it's a powerful weapon. I'm a crack shot if I do say so myself.

Rick drilled into me the four cardinal rules of carrying a firearm. All guns are loaded, even if you know they aren't; keep your finger off the trigger, straight along the frame unless you're on target and ready to fire; be sure of your target and what is beyond, and never point your weapon at anything you're not willing to destroy. He emphasized that what you practice is what you'll do in an emergency situation.

He told me about what happened to him when he was training at the academy. He'd gone home after a long, frustrating day, took the magazine out of his gun; a Sig Saur, and was dry firing from his couch when the phone rang. Automatically, he put the magazine back in the gun and answered the phone. When he got back to the couch he picked up his gun, pointed it at his brand new 27 inch color TV and blew it away.

Chapter 19

August 9, 1999
Marietta Ranch

I woke up after a night filled with horrid dreams, tired and grumpy. I had to drive into town to take care of some ranch business. It was evening when I drove back to the ranch. Daniel, my friend, teacher, and general manager of the Marietta, and Leon the head trainer had already left for the day. I unloaded the bags of bran and oats and stacked them in the feed shed. My muscles ached; nevertheless, the physical exercise was therapeutic. Sitting in front of the computer figuring out the ranch books can be a tedious chore.

I let the cold water of the shower rush over me for a long time and dried off in front of the fan. Stretching out on the bed I pulled a sheet up, leaving my feet and arms uncovered. I was asleep almost instantly. Not even the nightmares that had been plaguing me woke me up. The dreams used to be about Johnny's death, but since discovering the mutilated body of Lindy Dibbs, my dreams have incorporated other victims of violence. When I wake up, the nightmares don't end. They are all still dead.

Jennet Wilson, the first victim of the vicious predator in our community, was an eleven year old girl who'd been abducted while she was walking home from summer school. A suspect described as a man about six feet tall, wearing a blue shirt, cowboy hat, and boots was asking for help finding his lost dog. The kids who were with her said she got into a light colored pickup truck with a camper.

No one got a license number.

We searched the grape vineyards and citrus orchards near the school but found nothing. A week went by. I cried when I watched the Wilson family make a tearful appeal on television, begging the abductor to permit their daughter to come home. I knew there was very little chance that she would return alive.

Mukat's Heart: A Sunny Morgan Mystery

A hiker found the girl's body in an arroyo near Cabezon about a week later. Rick told me that the crime scene photos showed a small, unrecognizable form that used to be a laughing, happy child; her face smashed. Her body was wrapped loosely in a thin cotton sheet. Then Lindy Dibbs and Candy Hoggins; their bodies more horribly mutilated and no suspects.

Chapter 20

August 9, 1999
Marietta Ranch

Depression was threatening to eat me alive. I reached for the phone and punched in Carline's number. She answered sleepily. "Hello?"

"Caroline, this is Sunny. I'm sorry I called so late, but I have to talk to someone. I'm going out of my friggin mind."

"Sunny ... uh, let me get a cigarette." There was a brief pause. I could hear her exhale. "Okay, I'm back."

"God, Caroline, I'm in such a black mood. I just can't seem to stop crying."

"Lady ... what's the matter?"

"I don't know. It's just everything. I can't sleep ... nightmares."

"Johnny?"

"Yeah." I sighed. "That, and those girls."

"Sunny, I keep telling you to get out more, find someone. There's somebody out there for you. Listen, I'm throwing a party this weekend. I know just the guy. He's single, handsome, and is looking for Ms. Right." Caroline added hopefully, "Doesn't hurt that he's got money, too!"

"Caroline, a man's not going to help me. I feel so down. It's probably the weather. This old water cooler keeps throwing more humidity in the air. Can't get cool."

"Get a refrigeration unit, and then get a man. Trust me; I know what I'm talking about."

I knew I'd made a mistake calling Caroline. Her remedy for me is always a man. "Thanks for the invitation, Caroline. I'll get back to you about the weekend. Have to go. Talk to you later."

I remembered the last time I'd tried her solution. It didn't go very well. It was a little more than a year after Johnny had been killed. I was trying to lose myself in my job at the Marietta Ranch when I got a phone call.

"Sunny, this is Jerry Branson. Do you remember me?"

I thought for a moment, "You work with Rick at the department, right?"

"Yes. I hope I haven't caught you at a bad time. I know you're trying to settle into your new job at the ranch, but I was wondering if you would like to go out to a movie and maybe have dinner after."

I'd met Jerry at a Christmas party thrown by the local sheriff's station to benefit homeless children. Johnny had introduced us briefly and then escorted me onto the dance floor. I hadn't thought about Jerry since then. I guess he hadn't made much of an impression. Or maybe I was so in love with Johnny that no one else could have captured my interest.

I'd been feeling lonely lately and Jerry seemed innocuous enough, so I accepted.

"Yes, I think I would like that very much. Thank you."

"I'll pick you up at two and we can go to a matinee and then back to my place for dinner. My sister said she would love to meet you."

I was a little nervous because this would be my first date since Johnny's death. We went to the matinee and then to his house for dinner. Jerry was undemanding and fun to be with. He went into the kitchen, grabbed two bottles of Zima, and sat down next to me on a heavy, brown leather couch in the living room. I noticed a large portrait hanging over the fireplace. "Jerry, that's an interesting painting."

"Madge is a bit vain. She paid too much for it." Jerry stared at the painting and then turned to me with a smile. "Have you ever sat for a portrait, Sunny?"

"No."

"You should. You're very beautiful." I was flattered, but something was bothering me about the angry intensity of Madge's portrait. I couldn't put my finger on it, just something a little off in her expression. "Well, maybe sometime ... Jerry, I smell dinner cooking."

Jerry yelled out for his sister, "Madge, come out and meet Sunny."

A woman stomped out of the kitchen. Her hands were damp from washing dishes. She tentatively shook my hand and walked away without a word.

I wished I'd pursued the subject of the portrait; maybe if I had, Jerry wouldn't have antagonized his sister.

Jerry grumbled, "Madge, you ought to be more sociable."

She turned around, gave him a scathing look, and stalked into the kitchen.

Jerry tried to pass it off, but I could see he was really upset. "Don't pay any attention to my dear sister. She's a little peculiar sometimes." He grinned at me. "A typical old maid."

Madge was thin, almost anorexic, about five foot four. She had high cheek bones, a straight nose, and a beautiful, creamy complexion. She didn't need to wear makeup. Her face was framed by carefully dyed auburn hair tightly wrapped into a French roll. Her beauty was spoiled by a small, tight mouth and pale blue eyes that lacked warmth. I guessed that she was in her late forties.

"Sunny, I apologize. She's a nurse at Desert Dunes Hospital. Maybe one of her patients died."

"Don't worry about it, Jerry. Everybody has a bad day now and then."

Madge set the table for two, then produced a fantastic meal of stuffed pork chops, whipped potatoes with chives, and a tangy three-bean salad served on crisp lettuce leaves. I tried to get her to stay and share the dinner she had prepared, but she murmured that she had things to do, and walked quietly upstairs.

The weekend after my date with Jerry, Caroline asked me to babysit her daughter. Carrie and I were spending a quiet morning reading the Sunday paper when there was a knock on the door.

With my coffee still in my hand I opened the door. It was Jerry.

"Morning Sunny. I was just driving by and noticed that the gate was open. You have a cup of coffee for a weary deputy?" He looked over at Carrie and his face changed. The tired look around his eyes disappeared. He smiled at Carrie. "And who is this young lady?"

I've always thought Carrie was strikingly beautiful. Today she wore her long, dark-brown hair tied back in a ponytail. She's taller than most eleven year olds, and bright enough that she skipped a grade. The ADHD that she'd been diagnosed with as a kindergartner still affects her. She has trouble with writing assignments because she's thinking so fast she skips words, sometimes whole paragraphs. Carrie has a wry sense of humor and seems to get along better with adults than with her peers. Jerry and Carrie were chatting away while I washed the breakfast dishes.

"Hey Sunny, how would you and Carrie like to go for a drive up to Joshua Tree? We could stop for some takeout on the way."

"I promised Carrie that we would go for a ride this morning."

Carrie jumped up to help put the dishes away. "Sunny, it would be fun to go. Let's!"

"It's too hot for a picnic this time of year and the wildflowers are all gone."

Jerry cleared his throat, "Uh uh, I'll tell you what. Why don't you and Carrie go for your ride this morning? We'll go later this afternoon. Should be a little cooler in the high desert. Hey, it'll be fun."

"Oh Sunny, can we? I've never been there before."

Carrie had inherited her mother's determination minus the whine.

I gave in. "All right you two. Remember we have to be back by nine. Your mother said she'd pick you up then."

"No problem, Sunny. If we leave around four we can drive up there, have our picnic, enjoy the sunset, and be back in plenty of time."

We drove through Box Canyon to Interstate 10, through the Cottonwood Springs entrance and stopped at the visitors' center. For ten bucks we could spend all day. Jerry stayed in the truck while Carrie and I went inside. I studied the map of the park that the ranger gave me.

"Carrie, this is amazing. Check this out! It even shows where to find the animals and plants." I pointed out that Joshua Tree National Park includes parts of the Colorado and Mojave Deserts and has three different ecosystems.

"Uh huh. We studied about that in science class." She was excited when she approached the counter and saw the wildlife stationary for sale. "Sunny, I have to get some cards for Mom. Which ones do you like the best?"

"The endangered birds, but the wildflowers are beautiful, too."

Carried debated for a while and then finally decided on the hand-painted cards with desert wildflowers.

Jerry was waiting patiently for us. In no time we found a campsite close to a giant boulder that cast a long, cool shadow; just right for a picnic.

We walked a little way from the campsite. "Sunny, look!" She was pointing at a spot in the wash. "It's a Desert Star! Just like the one on the cards I got for Mom!"

"Where?" The wildflowers were so tiny that I had to crouch down near the sand to see them. That's what I call 'belly botany'. The desert is frugal, but there's no lack of beauty if you look closely enough. It was unusual to see wildflowers this time of year, but sometimes a little summer rain will encourage a few seeds to sprout out of season.

Carrie pointed to a top branch of a Palo Verde tree. "What kind of bird is that?"

"You're looking at a bird with its own family crest. It's a phainopepla." I chuckled as I remembered when Leon, the trainer at the Marietta, had said the same thing to me. He taught me to recognize the soft call of the phainopepla, a black crested bird that shows a flash of white when it flies.

While there was still enough daylight, I took a couple of photographs of Carrie standing on top of a spectacular granite monolith formed from some ancient up-thrust in the earth. As we hiked back to the truck, we surprised some quail chicks; small bundles of fluff scurrying in a line behind their mother. They were having a tough time negotiating some deep ruts made by a four-wheel drive vehicle.

"Those poor little babies." Carrie was incensed. "There's a sign right by the road that said, 'No Vehicles Beyond This Point.'"

"It's against the law, but some people don't care."

Carrie nodded her head. "Well, I hope someone catches them and puts them in jail!"

"Me too!" I vigorously nodded my head in agreement.

"Sunny, I have to take my meds and I'm getting hungry." Carrie's doctor prescribed Ritalin for her hyperactivity.

"I'll get the food out of the truck. We can look around some more later."

I set out the goodies on the picnic table and Jerry and Carrie wandered off for a walk. When they came back he and Carrie were holding hands. We finished off the whole bucket of fried chicken.

Jerry wiped a smear of chicken fat from his chin. "I would love to paint the two of you."

"I knew you did the composite sketches for the department, but I didn't know you painted. Do you use oils or watercolor?"

"Oh, oils mostly. Portraits. Remember the painting of Madge? It's one of mine. Maybe you would sit for me?"

"Well, maybe some time." I wasn't thrilled by the prospect of sitting for a portrait.

"Carrie, do you want some more chicken?" I mumbled while chewing on a particularly tasty drumstick.

"Couldn't eat another bite."

After dinner we watched the sun slide down behind the hills. I couldn't help it; I was nearly in tears. Johnny and I used to watch the sunset together. It wasn't the same with Jerry.

We took Carrie home. When I walked Carrie to the door, she whispered, "Jerry's a nice guy."

I wasn't surprised because they seemed to get along very well, but then she startled me.

"Sunny, you didn't have a very good time tonight, did you?"

"It's just hard for me to forget Johnny."

"Are you going to get married again?"

"Maybe someday. I'm not ready right now."

"That's good. Jerry's nice and all, but I don't think he's right for you." Carrie paused. "He wanted to paint my portrait. I told him I didn't want to. I could tell he was disappointed. I hope I didn't spoil it for you."

"Don't worry about it. We had fun today. That's what matters."

After we dropped Carrie off, we went to my place. Jerry invited himself in for a beer and before I knew it, he was all over me. When I pushed him off he got a strange look on his face, muttered under his breath that I was a frigid bitch, and stalked out the door.

Maybe he didn't think I heard what he called me, but I was truly surprised when he asked me out again. I told him I wouldn't date him again if he were the last male on the planet. Now, even Rick mentioned that whenever Jerry hears my name his lips purse up like he tasted a particularly sour lemon.

Chapter 21

July 1998

The day after my fiasco with Jerry, I found a quiet moment to talk to Daniel while we were walking around the ranch coyote-proofing the fences. The coyotes had been especially creative about getting into the aviary. They'd grabbed several unwary foul from the owner's exotic bird collection.

We'd finished patching a breech in the aviary screen. "Daniel, sometimes I wonder about myself."

Daniel smiled, "What do you wonder?"

"Oh, nothing I guess. I went with Carrie and a friend out to Joshua Tree yesterday. I was trying to get on with my life, but as it turned out, I was dredging up the past. I guess I overreacted to an innocent pass. He tried to kiss me and I acted like he was a rapist. I can't seem to respond physically to anyone anymore. I mean, he wasn't doing anything, not really. I kept thinking about Johnny. It wasn't fair to the guy."

Immediately Daniel metamorphosed from ranch manager to being my spiritual guide. "Pay attention to your inner self. If you didn't want to be intimate with this man, there had to be a reason. It's all right to say no. You don't have to …"

Daniel stopped in mid-sentence.

"What?" I could see that Daniel was troubled.

"I'm not sure, Sunny. Just that it probably isn't a good idea to take other people to those places where you went with Johnny. You'll have a hard time understanding your feelings."

"It was a special place for Johnny and me."

"Not just for you?"

"No, Daniel. I know we've talked about finding my own power place, but no, this was just a place where I'd been happy once. I thought it would make me feel good."

Daniel touched the tear that was threatening to fall down my cheek. "Did it make you feel good?"

"For a few hours I felt wonderful and then all the pain came back."

"I understand, Sunny. It's all right to remember your love for Johnny. I feel that way about Mary sometimes. That's probably it."

"What?"

"I'm not sure. I just felt a strong wave of anger and fear wash over me. Probably just thinking about Mary. I love her very much, but sometimes even when I'm with her I experience such a sense of loss. Maybe I'm just so happy I'm afraid I'll lose her." Not even Daniel could stop the events that would overwhelm us both.

Chapter 22

August 10, 1999
Marietta Ranch

"Leon, I have to talk to Sunny." Carrie whispered.

"What the devil?" Leon saw Carrie, her hair tousled, crouched behind the bags of horse feed in the storage shed. "Why didn't you go to the trailer?"

"Nobody was there."

"What's the problem, Carrie?" Leon recognized a runaway when he saw one. "No matter what the problem is, you shouldn't have run away. Your parents must be frantic."

"Leon, you don't understand. Lenny isn't my father. My real father is staying in town at a motel. He wants to take me away from Mom."

Leon offered his work-roughened hand to Carrie. "Come with me, and we'll find Sunny." Carrie reached for Leon's hand, stood up, and walked beside him. The worry lines on his face relaxed. "Lassie, Sunny'll get this sorted out."

I got up, wrapped my aging terrycloth robe around me. God, it was almost noon. Shadow scratched at the door and wagged her stubby tail. I peered through the spy hole in the door and saw Leon and Carrie.

"Sunny open the door!"

I turned the lock, took the chain off, and opened the door.

Leon had Carrie by the hand. She was out of breath. "Sunny, you have to hide me. There's a man going to hurt me."

I hustled Carrie inside. "Who's going to hurt you? Leon, what's going on here?"

Leon shook his head. "Not me, Sunny. You know I wouldn't hurt her. I found her in the feed shed." Leon explained what happened.

"You've caused a lot of worry, young lady. I just got a call from your mother!" I said severely, but with one look at Carries tear-stained face, I opened my arms and hugged her. "Come on in. We'll have something to eat and then you can tell me your troubles."

The tears disappeared. "Quesadillas?"

"Okay." Sandwiches weren't on the menu today. I found corn tortillas, butter, green onions, and cheddar cheese and took them out of the fridge. I like quesadillas better than tuna sandwiches anyway. "Here, Carrie, you grate the cheese." I gave her my old hand grater and the cheese. "Watch your knuckles. These are supposed to be vegetarian."

I chopped the green onions and put the skillet on medium heat with a little butter. When the butter was sizzling I put the tortillas in the pan, heated them, and turned them over. Carrie had the bowl of grated cheese ready. I put some cheese and onions on the tortillas and folded them. When the cheese melted I turned the tortillas over and cooked them until both sides were crisp. I took out a ready-made salad and some fresh squeezed lime juice. We sat down at the kitchen table to eat.

"Sunny, you knew my mom before she married my dad, didn't you?" Carrie asked between bites.

"Uh huh." Caroline had been my college roommate for a while. I let Carrie get to the point in her own way.

"Did you know someone named Greg Hanson?"

I looked at Carrie in surprise. "Yes, a long time ago. He was a friend of your mother's."

Carrie continued munching thoughtfully on her last quesadilla. "Well, he called the house. Mom and I picked up the phone at the same time. The man said he was Greg Hanson. I know I should have hung up but Mom sounded scared. I kept listening. He asked about me; how old I was. Mom told him I was ten. He started talking mean and told her not to lie. He knew I was eleven. He said that he had a better chance of being my father than Lenny did. He said he was staying at the Stars Motel and if Mom wanted to avoid a court battle, she'd better meet him there in an hour. Mom said she would." Carrie scrunched her eyes to keep from crying.

"When I went downstairs, Mom said that something had come up and she had to go out. She dropped me off at the store. She told me she would be back in a couple of hours. I know I should have said something, but I didn't want her to know I'd listened in. When she got back to the store she was in such a bad mood I didn't dare say anything. Sunny, I knew you'd listen to me. I'm sorry everyone is so upset, but if Dad isn't my dad, and Mom lied about it, what was I supposed to do?

"I put some stuff in my backpack and went over to Mrs. Benton's. She's a nice lady but she forgets things. She knows that I stay with you sometimes. Mom asked her to drive me over here once before. I knew she was going to visit her sister in Borego Springs and told her Mom wanted her to drop me off here."

The words just kept pouring out. Once Carrie had started talking, it seemed as though she couldn't stop. "He can't take me away, can he? I don't want to go with him. He sounded mean. He made Mom go see him. Sunny, I'm so scared."

I picked up the dishes from the table and took them to the sink.

"Carrie, I have to let your mom know that you're here."

She got a stubborn look on her face, "I can't go home, not until I know what's going on."

"All right, I'll ask your mom if you can stay here until we get this settled." I was beginning to understand why Caroline wanted Carrie to spend some time with me, but I was sure there was more to it than what Carrie had overheard. I picked up the phone and dialed. Caroline answered.

"This is Sunny. Carrie's with me at the ranch. She's safe. I need to talk to you."

"Sunny? You don't know the terrible things that have been going through my mind. What on earth was she thinking about, going off like that?"

"That's what I need to talk to you about. Carrie wants to stay here. Leon will look out for her. I'll tell you more when I see you."

I had just hung up the phone when it rang.

"Sunny ..."

"Rick, thank God you called. I have to talk to you. It's about Carrie."

"Is it an emergency?"

"Well, I think maybe ... She ran away from home and showed up here. Something's happened that's frightened her. I'm worried."

"Be there as soon as I can."

"Rick, I have to see Caroline first. I'll call you when I get back."

"Okay. You can call me at the station if I'm not home."

I asked Leon to keep an eye on Carrie while I worked out something with Caroline. It wasn't going to be pleasant. Thank the Gods for Leon. He was out in the barn showing Carrie a baby cottontail rabbit he'd rescued. Poor little thing had been attacked by a hawk but Leon said it was going to survive.

I was just about to leave for Caroline's condo when the phone rang again. It was Jerry. "Mrs. Morgan, I just heard that Carrie Costa turned up at your place. The Costas called the station. I'm concerned that you've been sheltering a minor and concealing her whereabouts."

"Jerry, don't be ridiculous! Talk to Rick, he knows what happened. I have to leave. I'm going to see Caroline right now."

"I strongly recommend you come in. If the Costa family files charges ..."

I screamed into the phone, "Jerry Branson, you're an idiot! Talk to Rick. I have to go now!" I slammed the phone down. It made me feel better, but I shouldn't have let that jerk get to me.

Chapter 23

August 10, 1999
Marietta Ranch

On the way to the Costas I tried to think about how to approach Caroline. I looked at myself in the rear view mirror. *Okay, Sunny Morgan, this has turned into a big mess and as usual, you're in the middle of it.* I drove into the parking lot and saw Caroline waiting impatiently. She hurried over to the driver's side window.

"Sunny ..."

"Caroline, before you say a word, Carrie heard your conversation with Greg."

"So that's it. I never should have let Greg know where we lived. I wrote to him just after Lenny and I were married. Stupid. Stupid!"

"Then, Greg is Carrie's natural father?" I frowned.

"I don't know. We were at a frat party. Our breakup was ugly. He stormed out and I got bombed out of my mind." Caroline hesitated, "Sunny, I was raped. I have no idea who her biological father is and I don't ever want to know. I only pray it isn't Greg.

"I thought about getting an abortion, in fact my parents practically delivered me to the clinic door. The doctor insisted that I get counseling before I had the procedure done and, much against my parents' wishes, I decided to keep the baby."

"It should be easy to prove that Greg's not the father. All you have to do is get a blood test."

"But that would involve Carrie, and I want to protect her. Lenny's been like a father to her. She loves him and he adores her."

"Well, it's a moot point now." I continued a little harshly, "You're going to have to tell her as much of the truth as you can. She needs to hear it from you. From what she told me of your conversation with Greg, she could be in danger."

Caroline moaned, "I know."

"Carrie said you went to meet him. What happened?"

Caroline started to cry. "Sunny, I was pregnant when I met Lenny. We fell in love, I mean really in love. When I married him it wasn't just because I was going to have a baby. Yesterday when Greg called me he threatened to tell Carrie that Lenny wasn't her father. He said the only way this was going to go away was if I gave him money. He wanted a hundred thousand dollars. He said if I paid him he promised to leave us alone. I don't know how Greg found out Lenny isn't Carries biological father, but I know he'll do what he says if I don't come up with the money."

"That's extortion. Report him and let the police take care of this."

"I'm afraid to do that. I don't have any proof and it will get worse if I cross him. I know what he's capable of."

"Have you told Lenny that Greg is threatening you? He needs to know what's happening," I said firmly. "In the meantime, let Carrie stay with me."

Caroline seemed confused. "Yes, Sunny, that would be best. I'll talk to Lenny. We'll get this straightened out," she stammered uncertainly.

Caroline tried to smile but wasn't doing too well. She was shaking when I tried to give her a consoling hug. She broke away from me and ran back toward the condo. I shrugged my shoulders helplessly, got in the Toyota, and drove back to the ranch.

Chapter 24

August 11, 1999
Marietta Ranch

I'd left a message on Rick's answering machine and called the station. I was still waiting to hear from him when Shadow began to bark softly. It was almost four in the morning. Something or someone was outside. Already tense, I grabbed my gun and opened the door. I heard some rustling and cautiously moved toward the sound. I'd just had night sights put on my Glock and the phosphorescent glow added to my courage. "Who's there? I have a gun and I know how to use it."

"Sunshine, it's me, Rick. Put the gun down. Jerry gave me your message. I came to check on you."

The gate to the ranch is always locked after dark. There's a phone box there, but it doesn't work. Rick had left his patrol car out by the gate and jumped over the fence.

"Rick, if you ever do this to me again I will shoot." I was appalled and embarrassed that I'd almost discharged my weapon without knowing what or at whom I was firing. I was furious with Rick. "What do you think you're doing? I could have killed you!"

"Relax. It isn't like you to be so careless. You should have stayed inside, I would have knocked."

"Someone's threatening Carrie!" Rick put his arm around me and gently pushed me inside.

Rick made his way to the coffee maker and poured two cups of hot, concentrated mud. He took a sip and poured it in the sink. "I'll make a new pot. Talk to me."

While Rick made coffee, I told him about the phone call that Carrie had overheard.

"Did Caroline tell you her side of the story?"

"Yes, it's worse than I thought. She's being blackmailed and she won't file a report. Carrie's in danger."

Chapter 25

August 12, 1999
Marietta Ranch

Daniel and Leon had already finished their early morning work when I finally went back to bed for an uncomfortable, restless sleep. I woke up at nine. Carrie was still sleeping. My indignant cat, Chowder, was sitting on my chest staring at me. I remembered her self-feeder was empty and I was out of dry food. I had to go to the post office in town to pick up some registered mail for the ranch anyway. My eyes were burning from lack of sleep as I turned on the shower full-blast.

I left a note for Carrie on the kitchen table letting her know I'd be back in a couple of hours.

Chowder stalked after me as far as the door then sat down, licked her paw, and cleaned her ears. Her human was finally taking care of business. I closed the door quietly behind me.

Leon walked by. "Morning Sunny. How's our girl this morning?"

"Sleeping. I have to go into town. Will you keep an eye out for her?"

"No problem. I'll check on her."

First stop was the post office and then the feed store. I bought a large bag of vitamin-rich crunchy bits for Shadow and some dry food for Chowder. Next stop, people food and the white flaked tuna that Chowder and I share. Half a can for tuna sandwiches, half for a kitty treat to make up for this morning. I got back to the ranch to find Shadow standing watch by the gate. She jumped into the back seat when I opened the door, put her head out the window, and barked joyously all the way to the trailer. At least somebody was pleased about the way this day had begun.

Leon met me at the trailer. "Sunny, Daniel took Carrie for a ride. He said they should be back before it gets dark."

"Thanks Leon. I'm glad she's getting her mind off her troubles."

Chowder sat like a statue on the porch. Shadow was just glad to see me, but food is a serious matter to Chowder and she scolded me for being late with breakfast. I dished out their culinary delights and poured myself another cup of coffee with two spoonsful of raw sugar and a packet of vanilla-flavored creamer. "Shadow, where did I stash the chocolate macadamia nut cookies?" Shadow couldn't care less as she scarfed up her kibble, but Chowder paused briefly and meowed. I hoped that she was being sympathetic.

Around noon Rick knocked on the trailer door. He had that no-nonsense, don't-mess-with-me look on his face. "You got a moment?"

"Sure. Carrie's out for a ride. What's wrong?"

"They found another body," he muttered, "not far from where the Wilson girl was discovered.

I was horrified. "That creep has to be stopped."

"We've had a lot of calls, but so far none of the leads have panned out. The victim is about the same age as the others, brown hair, wrapped in a sheet. Not much left of the face. Same MO as the other two."

"Rick, do they have any idea who it is?"

"No report of a missing girl that fits the description. The killer's getting more brutal every time. All of the victims' faces were viciously smashed with a blunt object, but this time he took out the girl's heart, put her right hand in blood and left a complete imprint on the sheet he wrapped around the body."

I almost gagged. "He took her heart?"

"Yes." Rick continued his gruesome narration. "The lab reports showed animal blood and hairs on the sheet. They didn't find that on the others. The coroner said there's evidence of sexual abuse and torture, but the cause of death was blows to the head and face."

I shivered, "Rick, there's a monster out there."

"No shit, Sherlock." Rick replied with a grim look on his face. "We're going to get this freak. He abducted and murdered the Wilson girl in June, the Dibbs girl in July. He carved out a piece of skin in the shape of a heart form her breast and now this one. We're looking at a pattern of increasing violence here. If I could just put the pieces together; I know I'm missing something right in front of me."

I started thinking about the dates. The first girl was abducted on June twentieth, right? Wasn't that the summer solstice?"

"Mm, no, that was the twenty-first. I don't buy into the idea of a cult, I think this is the work of one very disturbed man. He's an opportunist and he has time to stalk his victims. All the girls were within a year or two of the same age; they all had long brown hair. They were all Caucasian. He has specific tastes. He rapes them and then kills them. He smashes their faces and mutilates their bodies."

"Rick, it gives me nightmares. Those poor girls. They must have endured so much pain before they died."

"That's not the worst part. The coroner told me he suspects the creep must have a secure location to confine them for a few days before he killed them. This isn't general knowledge, but the autopsies showed all the victims had been drugged and raped repeatedly. Rick looked sick, "This time he ripped the girl's heart from her chest."

"My God!" I was horrified, "And he kept them alive for days before he killed them?"

"Do the math, Sunshine. The eighteenth of June was a Friday; the Wilson girl wasn't found until the following Saturday. She'd been dead for three or four days. The Dibbs girl was reported missing on the Fourth of July. Our training at Whitewater was on the tenth and she had been dead for a few days when we found her."

"What about this girl?"

"We don't know when she was abducted, but she's been dead for at least two days, maybe more."

"There has to be some way of catching this guy. Somebody has to know something!"

"The first two victims had some item of jewelry missing when we found them. There was a white circle on the latest victim's little finger where she'd worn a ring. He keeps souvenirs, and then there's the pendant with the broken chain that we found. I'm sure that has something to do with the murders."

"Have you got anything else? Hasn't anybody come forward with information?"

"There've been a few calls, but no solid leads. Except for the shovel you found, everything so far is linked to the victims, not the killer. No prints on the shovel. It could have come from any camper supply store."

"What about the pendant, Rick? That was an unusual piece of jewelry."

"We're trying to trace it."

"What about street fairs?"

"Good idea." Rick said grudgingly, and then changed the subject. "We don't have a murder weapon. No one has come up with enough information for a good composite. This lunatic seems to disappear into the sand and dust. I've about come to the end of my rope."

"Somebody must have seen something. He has to live somewhere, have a source of income. Damn it, there's got to be someone out there who knows him, maybe even suspects he could be the killer."

"Sunny, unless something turns up soon, another young life is going to be destroyed. You can count on it, and he just keeps getting better at what he does."

I could see that Rick was frustrated. The unsolved murders were weighing on him. My answer to frustration has always been food. "Rick, why don't we take a break. Let me fix you something. How about a beer and a tuna sandwich?"

"Sounds good, Sunshine. I'm bushed." Rick stretched out on the couch and I headed for the kitchen.

Chowder leaped up and sat on his chest waiting to be scratched under her chin. Shadow nudged at Chowder with a wet nose trying to get her to move, but Chowder wasn't having any of it. I looked in at the three of them. Rick was petting Shadow with one hand and scratching Chowder with the other, the very picture of harmony among beasts and man.

I felt ambushed by an inexplicable yearning which I quickly stuffed and tried to refocus my attention to spreading the tuna mixture on sourdough bread. I looked out the window and caught a glimpse of Leon carrying a bucket into the shed.

"Rick," I grumbled, "I can't believe how Leon spoils that burro. She's so fat now, she's about to burst."

There was no reply. Rick's eyes were closed. Shadow was sprawled on the braided rug beside the sofa and Chowder was expressing her content with a rumbling purr.

Carrie came flying through the door and nearly tripped on the steps as she rushed up to me. "Sunny, the sheriffs came and took Daniel. They said they wanted to talk to him. Why would they take Daniel?"

Rick sat up like a bolt of lightning had struck. "What?"

Carrie looked up at me as though her entire world had collided with the Hale-Bop comet. "We'd just let the horses go. They talked to him and then took him to the police car."

I gathered her up in my arms and stroked her hair until her sobbing quieted.

Leon came up to the trailer combing his red hair with his fingers the way he does when he's trying to figure out what to do with a stubborn colt. "Smitty told Carrie that Daniel didn't do anything wrong. He said they'd bring him back to the ranch."

Carrie appealed to Rick, "Can't you do something?"

"Don't worry." His tone belied his words. "They just need Daniel's help."

Leon went on, "It was Mitch Tolly and Dwayne Smith, you know, the deputies that came over with Patty Kimball to look at the horses. They said they wanted him to look at some photographs."

Rick was furious. "Damn it! I'm going down to the station. I'll find out what the hell is going on." He paused for a moment. "Leon, keep an eye on our girls."

"I'll be close by." Leon avoided answering directly. "Lady Gold's been acting peculiar and Durango is off his feed ..." Leon left hurriedly. Durango's an old pack mule; as ornery as Leon, and Lady Gold, his very pampered burro, is pregnant. She wasn't due for a while yet, but I knew Leon would rather deliver a foal tail-first than deal with Carrie or me right then.

"Don't worry about Daniel. He'll be back before you know it." I hugged Carrie again. "Your mom thinks it would be a good idea for you to stay with me for a couple of days while she takes care of the problem with Greg. He's a dangerous man, Carrie, and he was lying about being your father."

Carrie looked up at me with trusting eyes. "I knew you would help." She intertwined her fingers with mine and we retreated into the trailer. "Sunny, I'm tired. Those bags of horse feed weren't comfortable. I feel like one giant lump." She sighed, "I want to go to bed."

"You should have a little dinner first. I'll fix some chicken noodle soup. Soup and toast and a class of milk, real cold."

Carrie nodded. She ate the simple dinner as if she hadn't eaten for days, and curled up on the sofa. She was asleep before I could tuck her in. I pushed a strand of hair out of her face and kissed her lightly on her forehead. I turned on the security lights and went out to find Leon.

He was brushing Lady Gold when I found him. "Leon."

"What? Who?" Leon turned around. He had a strange look on his face, something between anger and fear. "Oh, it's you. Sunny, you shouldn't creep up on a person like that."

"Sorry, Leon, I didn't mean to startle you." Leon's reaction surprised me. I was used to his gruffness, but he wasn't usually so tense. "Leon, I want you to keep an eye out. Carrie could be in danger. If you see anybody that you don't know around the place, tell me."

"I don't like this, Sunny! Daniel, a more honest man than you could find, gets picked up by the cops, and now you're telling me Carrie's in danger here on the Marietta. What the hell's going on? I have enough to do around here without all this mysterious mumbo jumbo. Cops all around and now even sweet little Carrie hiding out. To top it off, yesterday I got a telegram from the owners telling me they were letting me go. I called Mr. Marietta himself to ask why. He didn't know anything about it. He called me back and said that the telegram was bogus."

"Who would have done a thing like that?"

"I've made some enemies over the years," Leon looked away, "probably just somebody playing a vicious trick."

"Leon, have you been inside the bunkhouse today?"

"No. Why?"

"When I was making my rounds, I found the door unlocked."

The owners used the so-called bunkhouse for guests when they were on the ranch. It had a kitchenette, a wet bar, and three bedrooms. The living area was set up with a computer for guests to use and an elaborate entertainment system as well.

The owners hired a commercial cleaning crew that came to maintain both the ranch house and the bunkhouse.

Leon was perplexed, "The maintenance people were here yesterday. They may have left the door unlocked."

The cleaning crew had never left the doors unlocked before, and besides, I checked the bunkhouse yesterday. I was getting worried. "I'm going back to the trailer. I don't want Carrie to be alone."

I started to walk away. "Leon, I think you better check the bunkhouse. See if anything's missing. Stop by the trailer before you leave. Be careful Leon. I'm getting a bad feeling about what's happening here."

"It's getting dark. Maybe I should stay here tonight." Leon seemed about to say something else and then hesitated.

"Thanks, but it isn't necessary."

"It would make me feel better." Leon was watching me carefully.

At first I resisted the offer, but then I thought about Carrie's safety. "All right, if you want to stay."

"Consider it done."

I walked cautiously back toward the trailer on alert for any unusual sound. "I wish I'd brought my gun with me." Even with security lights there were too many shadows between the horse barn and my trailer.

Chapter 26

August 13, 1999
Twin Palms Sheriff Station

Deputy Mitch Tolly walked into the Sheriff Station wiping his face with the back of his hand. "Hey Jerry, why's it so hot in here?"

"The air conditioning expert says the compressor is defunct. He didn't have the right parts on the truck. Promised to be back two hours ago." Jerry Branson turned an oscillating fan to high speed. He grabbed a small brass replica of *The End of the Trail* and put it on top of a pile of reports as they rattled, shifted, and started to sail off his desk.

Mitch grunted, "You'll see that guy in a week or two if you're lucky. Everybody in the desert is trying to get cool. Haven't seen you lately. What's shaking?"

"Same'o, same'o, Mitch. Had a few vacation days and went up to Hemet Lake to do some fishing. Not much biting though. Must be the hot weather."

"That place has really changed. Didn't used to be so many people camping there, even in the summer. I used to take my boat to the lake. You ever been to Grapevine Springs up around Sugarloaf?"

"Nope, hiking isn't my thing. Now, four-wheeling, that's the way to go."

"Rick told me he and Sunny rode the old Guadalupe trail from Sugarloaf down to Grapevine and then to Cactus Springs all the way to the desert." He watched Jerry carefully. "They seem to be quite the couple these days."

"Mitch, you got it all wrong. Sunny doesn't give a damn about Rick, she's just using him. I went out with her a couple of times. She was hot to trot, let me tell you. We had some fine times."

"Sure, Jerry. So why aren't you two getting it on now?"

"She's too pushy. Wants to get married and all. Not for me, let me tell you. I let her down easy. Nobody's gonna trap this guy."

"How's dear sister Madge these days?"

"She's her same bitchy self. Works all the time. Never has a minute to help me. I moved out of my apartment because I couldn't afford the rent, my truck needs major work, and it doesn't look like I'm getting a raise this year. I asked my dear sister if I could stay in my old room for a while so I could save some money. She told me to go to hell. It's a good thing I found a place up in Yucca Valley. The rent's cheap but it's a long commute. Gas is expensive. I need a new vehicle. Don't know how much longer my old truck's going to make it. You'd think family would stick together."

Mitch smirked, "You and your sister do aggravate one another. What burr does she have up her tail this time?"

Jerry scoffed, "It's a long, boring story, not worth telling. She's just a bitch, that's all."

"Did you hear they identified the latest Whitewater Canyon victim?"

"No. Missed roll call this morning. Jeff was really PO'd at me. He's been riding me for months, ever since Daniel Martinez and I got into it over the Mary Canyon murder. An informant claimed he saw Daniel's brother, Michael, running away from the scene. I went to the Martinez residence and made the arrest. Maybe I was a little rough on the guy. He's good for the murder. Admits to having been there even if he denies killing her. The department should have given me a medal. Instead Jeff gave me a bad evaluation and threatened to put me on leave without pay. Said I had three months to improve. I'm thinking about asking for a transfer."

"Yeah, well don't let it get to you. Jeff's always been soft on minorities. I had a run in with him myself. He'd never let a white man get away with assaulting one of his men, but he wrote me up for using excessive force on a Mexican coyote trying to evade arrest when we stopped his van full of illegals. At least ten got away from us. There was some bad press. I had to apologize, but nothing came of it."

Jerry nodded, "Yeah, I heard about that."

Mitch continued, "Anyway, like I was saying, they got the murdered girl's prints and ran them. Seems she came from a little place up in the mountains called Pine Cove. She was hitching up to

Idyllwild the last time she was seen. Her friends said she wanted to go to a rave party and didn't have a ride. Kids can be real stupid."

"Sounds like a loser."

"Yeah, she's been in juvy twice. Shoplifting. Last time she was busted at the Palm Desert Mall; maybe you processed her. Name was Candy Hoggins."

"Don't remember the name."

"Lived with her dad. Some dad, he didn't even know she was gone. Thought a thirteen year old should be able to stay by herself for a few days. He spent the weekend in L.A. with a girlfriend."

"Well, I bet he thinks different now."

"Yeah, he and some of the other parents are organizing to raise reward money to get the Whitewater Canyon killer."

"Every one of those girls was asking for trouble and they got it."

Mitch was taken aback; "Jerry, nobody deserves that ..." He walked away with a troubled expression.

Jerry quickly picked up the phone.

Chapter 27

Shaggy Pines Ranch

Earl stomped out of the shed wiping his hands on a rag. He was followed by the cowering black and tan German shepherd puppy. "Hey man, slow down! You're making too much dust."

Handy jumped out of the green Ford. "Earl, he growled, "Where's Tobias? He was supposed to have been back hours ago. I should have known better than to let him make a run down to Mexicali. He can't stay away from booze and whores. Toby's got no class, doesn't care where he dips his wick. Now me, I like 'em young and tender, but clean, you know. The last time Toby went to Mexicali for a weekend he got so drunk he screwed a fifteen year old slut that probably had every disease known to man. The little whore's father raised hell when Toby wouldn't pay up after he'd screwed her. He landed in jail down there. It cost me big time to get his dirty carcass back to the States."

"Handy, I got some bad news. Be better if Toby was in a Mexicali jail. He never made it back this time because he got stopped by the CHP. Asshole panicked and shot a cop. He's busted for attempted murder and possession with intent. Got my truck impounded and now the cops are looking for me! No way Toby's gonna make bail this time."

"Shit! That lousy turd. He can't keep his mouth shut. That cuts it. We've gotta split."

Earl whined, "I just got everything set up here."

Handy sneered, "Poor Earl, you're going to have to leave your mountain paradise." He shook his head angrily, pushed his way past Earl, and stalked into the farmhouse. He grabbed a battered old suitcase, and started stuffing it with what was left of the money they'd made from the last deal. "Earl, get the guns. Roll 'em up on that rug. Leave everything else. Here, put this in the car."

Handy went into the barn. A few minutes later he came out and ordered, "Earl, put those doors back across the entrance. Move it!"

"Gawd, Handy. Yud think yuh was my mother."

"Yeah? Get going or you'll wish I was your mother."

"What about my dog?"

"Forget the damn dog. Get in the car. If we're lucky, Toby hasn't spilled his guts yet."

Handy roared up to Highway 74, slowed briefly for the cattle guard, made a left turn, and sped down the winding mountain road toward Palm Desert. "I've got a place down there where we can stay for a couple of days. I have to take care of some business and then we can head out for L.A."

"What about the lab? We got all our stuff stashed out there. You gonna leave everything?"

"Look behind you. I started a couple of little fires. There won't even be a fingerprint left. We'll get the money to set up again somewhere else. It's too big a risk to keep the operation going at Toby's place." He slammed one hand down on the dashboard in exasperation. "It was a sweet set up while it lasted, but the trick to staying out of prison is getting out clean. We have to dump this piece of junk and pick up some new wheels. Toby can't tell anybody what he doesn't know."

"He knows who we are."

Handy stared at Earl with an ugly grin. "He knows who you are."

Handy let Earl sweat for a few minutes and then relented. "We'll get new identification, no sweat. I know a guy in the desert who makes his living faking ID's for wetbacks. Just a couple of days and we'll be out of here free and clear."

"Handy, I'm hungry. Let's stop at Mickey D's for some chow."

"First we have to get some new wheels"

Handy swung into a used car lot. He talked briefly with the salesman and came back with a new set of car keys. "Earl, get our stuff out of the car and put it in that one over there." He pointed at a black car with Oklahoma plates sitting off to the rear of the lot.

Earl did what he was told; no argument this time. When they were back on the road, Earl whined, "Handy, I gotta have sumthun to eat."

"Can't stop thinking about your stomach for a minute." Handy smirked as he pulled into the drive-thru lane.

Handy and Earl drove up to the motel in a black Honda Civic. Earl grabbed the cardboard box with burgers and fries and a large Coke. Handy carried the bottle of Jack Daniels. "Here," Handy said, tossing him the keys. "Open the door."

Earl nearly dropped the box, but grabbed the key. "Handy, knock it off!"

"What's the matter, Earl, no manual dexterity?"

"Shit man, you had a free hand." Then he saw the look on Handy's face and put the key in the lock.

When they got inside Handy put the bottle down on the dresser by the television. He un-wrapped a plastic cup and poured a good measure of Jack into it. Earl closed the door and put Handy's hamburger and fries on the small round table.

"This is all right!" Earl turned on the television. "They get cable? I haven't watched a good movie in months."

"Yeah, they have cable."

Earl started flipping channels until he found a Clint Eastwood spaghetti western. He flopped on the double bed farthest from the door and un-wrapped his cheeseburger. "This is the life. A good burger and a movie. I've been dreaming about this. Living up there in the middle of nowhere, I got to feeling a little deprived. Toby's idea of a good meal was stewed squirrel. A little of that Jack in my Coke and I'll be a happy man."

"Get it yourself."

"Sure Handy. Didn't mean for you to …"

Part way through the movie Handy got up. "Earl, I have to go out. I'll be back in a few."

"Sure Handy. I got nowhere else to go. See you later."

Handy went out the door and down the stairs to the parking lot. He opened the trunk to the Honda, unrolled the rug and slipped Earl's Saturday night special into the waistband of his slacks. He swaggered across the street to a payphone and put some change in the coin slot and punched in the familiar numbers. The phone rang four times before the answering machine picked up.

Handy snarled threateningly, "Caroline, I know you have the money. Don't play games with me." Handy clicked off. He took a business card from his wallet and dialed again. "Pete, this is Handy, I need some new ID. Can you get it done by tomorrow?"

"Got a driver's license with your mug on it?"

"Pete, you got it on file from the last time. Just make me up a new one."

"How soon do you need it?"

"Like yesterday!" Handy snarled into the receiver.

"Um … new license and SSN in 24 hours. It's going to cost you five big ones."

"No problem, Pete. You just produce the goods."

"Be ready like I told you. Anything else?"

"No. I'll see you tomorrow."

Handy put the receiver back in its cradle and strolled over to the Starlight Bar across the street from the motel. He ordered a pitcher of beer and relaxed in a booth facing the front window. With an ugly grin he glanced at his watch and walked deliberately back to the motel room. The bottle of Jack was half empty. Earl lay snoring, passed out on the bed, a shoot-out blaring on the television. "You never could handle hard liquor." Handy said softly. He took out the gun, wiped it, put it in Earl's limp hand, and pulled the trigger, putting a bullet into Earl's temple.

"Sorry, Earl." He grabbed the bottle of Jack, what was left of his hamburger and fries, and went out the door. A frowzy woman sauntered out of the adjacent room. "Can't you guys keep it down over there?"

"Sorry lady. Here, take this as an apology for your trouble." He handed her the half empty bottle of Jack.

"Oooh! Classy! Dude, you want to join me?" She rolled her eyes toward her room.

She looked back hopefully but Handy was already on his way down the stairs planning his next move. He mumbled to himself, "Just one more thing to take care of and I'm outta here."

The good guys were winning on the television gun battle as Handy got into his Honda and drove away.

Chapter 28

August 13, 1999
Twin Palms Sheriff Station

Jerry knocked on the door to Jeff Newhowser's office. "Captain, we just got a call that connects the man who shot the CHP officer with a fire that burned several hundred acres of brush up on Pinyon. I talked to the arson investigators. They said Tobias Black, aka Toby Black, owns a couple of acres where the fire started. Their investigation proved that the fire was deliberately set, but Black's no good for the arson. He was already in custody. They did find evidence of a meth lab on his property. Matthew Patterson from the Narcotics Task Force thinks there's a chance we can get him to rat on his partners. He's already sweating the attempted murder charge and his lawyer quit on him."

"Tell Matt to go ahead. See if Black will give them up. Let him think that his buddies dropped a dime on him." Jeff put a stack of papers into his out box.

"Will do."

"Did Mitch get anything out of Daniel Martinez?"

Jerry was startled, "About what?"

"He was tipped that Martinez knew something about the latest Whitewater Canyon killing. Mitch and Smitty went out to the Marietta Ranch and brought him in for questioning."

"I don't know anything about that."

Jeff's face was unreadable. "Hmm ... I guess you better get back to work."

Chapter 29

August 13, 1999
Twin Palms Sheriff Station

Smitty nervously rubbed his fingers against his thumbs as Mitch began the interrogation.

"Daniel, we want you to look at some pictures. They aren't pretty, but we think that you might be able to help us."

Mitch Tolly leaned aggressively toward Daniel and laid out several photos on the table. "Do you recognize the designs?"

"The toad and the zigzag lines are Indian designs, if that's what you're getting at," Daniel grumbled, "but the Cahuilla never cut them on children and they don't use children's blood to make handprints."

"You admit that those designs are Cahuilla in origin?"

"I didn't say that. Whoever did it doesn't know anything about Indian culture. We love and protect our children." Daniel stared at the pictures. He shuddered involuntarily. "That abomination has to be a personal thing, something dredged up from a very sick mind." Daniel continued forcefully, "It probably means something, but it doesn't have any significance to me other than utter horror."

Mitch was insistent, "Come on, Daniel, we know you aren't telling everything you know about this."

"I can't help you, at least not from what I see in these photos. Only a lunatic could do that to a child. He obliterates their faces, leaves their handprints; uses their bodies like an artist's canvas and discards them carelessly in the desert like trash. It's disgusting. You should talk to a psychiatrist, not to me."

"How about this?" Mitch threw the pendant found by Lindy Dibbs' body down in front of Daniel. "We know there was a guy selling these things at your Indian pow wow."

"Then you should talk to him," Daniel said angrily. When he reached out to pick up the amulet, a dark strand of mist coiled around his hand like a snake. Daniel dropped the amulet on the table as if he had been burned, his face twisted by revulsion. It was the same design that had been carved on Mary's door.

Smitty noticed the look but misunderstood the cause. He hadn't seen anything unusual, but he instantly noticed Daniel's alarm. "Daniel, I'm not saying it was one of your people that did this thing. We only wanted your input."

"That's exactly what you're trying to imply."

"No Daniel, it's just that we haven't found any leads. We were hoping you might notice something we missed," Smitty said carefully. "You helped us once before when we found that carving on Mary's door. This looks remarkably similar."

"Yeah, and you arrested me, threw me in jail; my fiancée was murdered and now my brother is in danger of being executed. The murderer is still out there. You bastards didn't listen to me then; you used me. I have my work at the community center and the ranch. I have no intention of getting involved with this case. Even if I could see something, it won't change anything. I told you before that an Anglo was responsible." Daniel continued to speak but his words were less certain. "His sickness doesn't belong to me or my people."

Smitty urged, "Daniel, we have to stop this guy. He's killed and mutilated three young girls. If there's anything you can tell us, it might help us get him before the number increases."

Daniel gave Smitty a dark glance. "I can't help you." He stared unwillingly at the pendant, and again the vision enveloped him. Angry red claws slashed at his questioners' throats. One bloody talon snaked toward Daniel. He shook his head as if he were trying to persuade himself that this had nothing to do with him, but in truth he was desperately trying to push the vision away. "There is something," Daniel's face was pale. "There's a legend in our tradition that Frog 'witched' the Creator, Mukat, because he brought death to the people. The Creator sickened and died and Coyote stole his heart and ate it. Even today the frog or toad is used by some to 'witch' people, but," Daniel pointed to the amulet, "Maybe …"

"Maybe what?" Smitty asked skeptically.

Daniel regained his composure. "Anyone could read about that. What those photos show is not the work of a medicine man, of that I am certain.

"That helps us a lot," Mitch sneered.

Smitty noticed that Daniel hadn't answered his question, but before he could pursue it, Jeff strode angrily into the interrogation room with Brad following closely behind. He was gritting his teeth, trying to control his temper. "Daniel, Brad is going to drive you home. I know you didn't want to get involved, but thank you for coming down. If you think of anything that can help us, call."

"Yeah." Daniel's face was resolute and without expression. "Jeff, talk to my brother Tony. He knows about such things. I know you don't believe in it, but dark magic can unloose real demons." Daniel grimaced, "Antonio might be able to tell you something about that amulet."

"I've heard of him. He's a shaman, isn't he?"

"Some people call him one, but he was never properly trained in the way of the Great Spirit. Antonio has a sly conniving guide. He's proficient with black magic and uses evil spirits to gain his own ends. A true shaman would never do that. He hates me, my family, and everyone I care about. He's involved in this somehow. I think he would rather have seen Mary dead than married to me. He's the only one I know who uses the image of a toad in his magic." Daniel had said more to Jeff than he'd intended. "Now, if you are done with me, I need to go home."

Mitch and Smitty were left behind in the interrogation room listening incredulously while Daniel shared this extraordinary information with Jeff.

"Jeff, take what I am telling you seriously. He has power. He's testified under oath that he thinks Michael was responsible for Mary Canyon's death. She was my fiancée. I loved her. *No* one else in my family would have hurt her."

"I'll look into it, Daniel."

Daniel turned around and looked straight into Mitch's eyes. "If you had half a brain you'd realize that there really is a struggle between good and evil, and you're going to have to take sides one of these days."

"Daniel ..." Mitch started to explain, but Jeff interrupted. "Let's go, Daniel. He doesn't understand. It's not part of his world."

"We're just trying to find this guy." Brad put his hand on Daniel's shoulder. "I wish you weren't so angry. It wasn't our fault your brother went to prison."

Daniel exhaled slowly, "Michael didn't do it, you know. He didn't use drugs and he isn't the one who butchered Mary. He didn't even carry a knife. The informant who placed him at the scene never came forward. My brother said that Mary was already dead when he got there and I believe him."

"A jury found him guilty. He admitted he was there. He was covered with blood; hers and his. Accept it. I'll take you back to your truck." Brad had a pained expression on his face. "I know you don't want to believe it, but all the evidence points to Michael."

"Brad, I have heard you. Let's go. I don't need you to lecture me."

They went out together, a temporary truce acknowledged.

Jeff waited until Daniel and Brad were out of earshot. "Mitch, what was the point of bringing Daniel Martinez down to the station? You don't think he has anything to do with this, do you?" There was a dangerous edge to his voice.

"Maybe not, Jeff, but the designs the killer cuts on those girls look a lot like the carvings we found on the door at the scene of the Mary Canyon murder. I think he knew a lot more about that killing than he ever told us." Mitch responded unhappily.

"It's a closed case Mitch. Drop it!" Jeff ordered abruptly.

"OK, Captain. I'll let it go, but I still think Daniel knows something. You should have heard him talking about letting monsters loose."

"I did. Something for you to think about, Mitch. We're in law enforcement, and if anyone could believe in monsters on the loose, at least human ones, we can."

Smitty remained quiet waiting for the ax to fall.

Mitch couldn't stop himself from wisecracking. "Yeah, but it didn't sound like he was talking flesh and blood."

Jeff continued in a firm voice, "You know that Daniel is a respected leader for his band. Even if you thought he knew something, there was a better way to ask for it. You didn't have to pick him up and bring him in like a suspect."

Smitty nodded his head in agreement, but didn't speak.

Jeff didn't say anything more. He knew Mitch was a dedicated officer. Unfortunately he had no sensitivity when it came to dealing with people of other cultures. He made a note to find out about sensitivity training.

Mitch went out the door muttering to himself about political correctness being more important now than busting criminals.

Jeff turned to Smitty, waiting for an explanation. "Smitty?"

"Jeff, we got an anonymous tip that we should talk to Daniel. Jerry took the call and passed it on to us. We were just following up on the information. I know Mitch has a thing about Daniel, but it wasn't his idea. We were doing our job; there wasn't anything else to it."

"Okay, Smitty, but I don't like the way it was handled."

Chapter 30

August 13, 1999
Marietta Ranch

Greg Hanson was beginning to panic. It was taking too long to get the money. It was just a matter of time before the cops made the connection between Handy Miller and Earl. He had to get the new ID and get out of here. He'd planned it carefully, but things were beginning to fall apart. The Costas had a profitable business. They owed it to him. He knew they wouldn't have trouble getting the cash. "Damn that Caroline!" The expression on Greg's face was deadly. "Bitch! She'll pay for this."

He picked up the phone and angrily punched the buttons. "Time to put the screws to her."

"Hello."

"Caroline, I want my money now, in cash! I know you can get it." Greg's voice was harsh. "You want to get me off your back; you're going to have to pay for it."

"You're not getting any money from me Greg Hanson! Lenny knows what you're trying to do. Leave my family alone or I'll call the cops."

"You think you know it all, but you don't. Remember that last little party in Isla Vista? I was there with my buddies. We did have one fine time that night; a real pussy party."

"You bastard."

"Think about it, I'm not the one who's a bastard. Get the money or you're going to be very, very sorry, Caroline. You and your whole little family are going to be sorry."

Caroline slammed the receiver down. Her face was pale with anger and dread when she finally called Lenny at the shop.

"Greg called again."

"That bastard! We've got to make sure that Carrie is safe!"

"Lenny Carrie is staying with Sunny for a few days."

"I know, but is she ...?"

"She's fine, Lenny, she's fine. I have to talk to you though. Can you close early and come home?"

"I'll leave as soon as I close out the register."

"I love you Lenny."

"I love you too, Sweets."

When Lenny got home he unlocked the door and turned the knob only to find the chain was fastened on the inside. "Lina! It's me, Lenny. Open the door!"

Caroline unfastened the chain. The moment Lenny came through the door Caroline fell sobbing into his arms. Lenny walked her to the couch and sat down beside her. "Lina, what's wrong? Carrie's all right, isn't she? She's safe with Sunny?" he questioned.

"Yes." The tears started to subside. "Lenny, when Greg called, he threatened to take Carrie away from us. He demanded a lot of money to leave us alone."

Leonard's face was grim. "I thought that was all behind us. Where's he staying? I'll have a conversation with him that'll make him wish he'd never heard of my family!"

"Don't, Lenny! Sunny says to let the police take care of him. He could be dangerous."

"This is personal." Lenny grabbed Caroline's shoulders roughly. "This is something I have to do, nobody else. Where's he staying?"

"Stars Motel. He's in room twenty six." Caroline was shaking.

"I'm sorry." Lenny put his arms around Caroline. "Sweets, don't worry about this. I'll take care of Greg Hanson. Now you go wash your face. Carrie'll be back home in no time. I love you, and I love Carrie like she was my own child. Nobody's going to spoil that."

Lenny went into the bedroom and took his nine millimeter from the top shelf of the closet. He left without saying good-bye to Caroline.

Lenny drove up to the Stars Motel, parked, and walked up to room twenty six. He knocked. There was no answer but the door was not firmly closed. Lenny pushed the door. "Greg?" He went inside. No one responded. The television was still blaring. In the dim light, Lenny saw the bloody head on the pillow. He went over to the bed, checked for a pulse even though it was obvious that the man was dead. He didn't recognize him, but it had been many years since he had seen Greg, and the face was distorted by the bloody gouge caused by the bullet. *Good*, he thought. *Somebody did it for me.* He took out his cell phone and punched in 911. He reported the body, wiped the door handle, and pulled the door shut.

Perspiration poured down Lenny's face. He knew that he should have stayed until the police arrived, but there were too many questions that he couldn't answer. He drove home to find Caroline more upset than ever. "Lina?"

She put her finger over her mouth to signal Lenny to be quiet. The phone was in her shaking hands. "What do you want?"

"Caroline, don't talk, just listen. You better get me the money or you'll be sorry." The phone went dead.

"Lenny, it's him again. We have to get the money!"

"What?" Lenny was stunned. He almost blurted out that Greg was dead. But if that wasn't Greg Hanson in the motel room, then who was it?

"Lina, call Sunny. I'm sure Carrie's safe. He doesn't know where she is."

Caroline's face smoothed a little, but the tears were still forming in her eyes as she dialed Sunny's number. A man's voice answered.

"Rick?"

"No, ma'am, this is Sergeant Neely. Who is this?"

"Caroline Costa. May I speak with Sunny please?"

"Are you Carrie Costa's mother?"

"Yes. What's wrong? Has anything happened to Carrie?"

"Ma'am, are you calling from home?"

"Yes. What's happening there? Where's Sunny?"

"A deputy is on route to your residence right now. He'll explain everything then. Please remain there until the deputy arrives."

Caroline's face was white and her hand shook as she replaced the receiver. "Oh God! I knew it. A sheriff answered the phone. He wouldn't tell me anything. Greg kidnapped Carrie, I'm sure of it. There's a deputy coming. We can't say anything. Greg will kill her. What if he's watching the house and sees the sheriff's car?"

"Caroline, there's no way Greg could know where Carrie is," but Lenny's face had a look of panic. "What if it's something else? What if it's that madman? Those little girls ..."

"Don't even think that! Lenny, it has to be Greg. We'll get Carrie back. We just need to come up with the money."

Chapter 31

August 1999
Stars Motel

The Stars Motel was in an unincorporated part of the county served by the Sheriff's Department. Mitch Tolly and Dwayne Smith responded to the 911 call.

They pushed on the glass door to the dingy office where the day clerk sat reading about flying saucers and alien babies. There was a sour smell of cigarette butts and unwashed clothes. "We got a call that you have a dead man in twenty six," Mitch growled, flashing his badge. The clerk scratched his grimy fingers through oily, dirt-brown hair. He was thin; his face pimply, a wisp of mustache unevenly trimmed straggled above his lip. He reluctantly put the magazine down on his desk, pulled out the master keys, and tossed them to Mitch and started reading again.

"Don't get too comfortable," Mitch snapped, "We'll have some more questions for you."

"Sure, anytime." The clerk looked up at Mitch. "I ain't goin' nowhere."

Mitch and Smitty walked around the brown stucco building to the metal stairs going up to the second floor walkway. A short, stout woman, about forty-five, wearing a Budweiser tee-shirt with the sleeves rolled up, was just coming out of room twenty three. Her hair was bleached blonde, shaved on one side, and there was a tattoo of a large red rose on her left upper arm. She had a motel ice bucket in her hand and gave the deputies a brief glance before she tromped down the stairs.

Mitch pounded on the door of room twenty six. "Sheriff! Open the door!" He turned the key in the lock and pushed the door open with his foot, gun ready. Smitty went in, swept the room with his .38, paused briefly to confirm that the man on the bed was dead, and checked out the bathroom. Except for the corpse, the place was empty. A gun was lying next to the left hand and bits of bone, splatters of brain, and blood were darkening on the pillow, blending in with the orange and red flowered print bedspread.

"Smitty, looks like this guy blew himself away. Call it in"

"We have a possible suicide at the Stars Motel. Request assistance."

Mitch secured the scene.

Ernie and the crime scene detectives arrived. "Well, Mitch, you got another beauty for me. You interviewed anyone yet?"

"No. Smitty went down to question the desk clerk. We haven't gotten anything on the victim yet. Just waiting for the experts." Mitch smiled broadly.

"Mitch, you're a man who loves his work." Ernie chuckled as he put on his latex gloves.

Smitty strode belligerently into the motel office. "I have some questions for you."

The clerk glanced up briefly and continued to turn the pages of the tabloid.

Smitty snarled, "Put the damn magazine down!"

"Okay! Okay!" he smirked and stuffed the magazine into the right hand drawer of the desk, and looked at Smitty's ID which was almost in his face. "Deputy Smith, what do you want to know?" He tried to smile, but couldn't quite loose the sneer.

"Your name and a home address where we can find you when you're not," Smitty paused, "working."

"Hey, man, I live here. Free rent."

"Your name."

"Otis Grimes."

"You on the desk all day?"

"Yup, I'm always on the desk. Someone comes in, I register them. If I'm not here, they don't get a room."

"Tell me about the guy in twenty six."

"A few days ago this fella came in. Wanted a room. Drove up in a big green station wagon. He was here for two days, in and out, and then he was gone for a day. Paid two weeks in advance, so I didn't care where he went. When he came back he was driving a black Civic and he had another guy with him. They went to the room. The guy who rented the room left in the Civic. The other guy never came out. I don't worry about the guests; they come and go. As long as I get the money, they can drink themselves to death for all I care. When their money runs out, they're out."

"You get a name?"

"Yeah. I'll get the registration card. Hang tight for a minute." He pawed through a file box. "John Smith."

"Surprise, surprise. Can you describe him?"

"Blonde hair, kinda paunchy, a nice dresser though. About average height. Not too much to tell, he looks like a dozen others that come in and outta here every day. Haven't seen him since late this morning."

"You hear anything from that room?"

"Naw, there weren't any calls in or out. I don't go snooping 'round; not good for business, but you can ask Tiny. She checks out anything wearing pants. Room twenty three. She may know something. The maids make up the rooms early. Theresa already cleaned twenty six before those two drove in."

"What about the other guy?"

"He was kinda tall, had a mustache; dressed like a cowboy, on the lean side."

"Think of anything else?"

Otis hesitated, "Well, yeah … there was one thing … this guy in a black Mercedes drove in, got out of his car and went up there. Wasn't there more than five minutes. Took off like someone was chasing him."

"I thought you didn't snoop."

"Well, sometimes I notice things." Otis admitted. "This guy was out of place, you know, looked like money."

"Describe him."

"In his thirties or early forties. Nice suit. Didn't get a look at his face; but his car, now that's different. Had one of those special license plates. 'Costa 1'. I remember because I thought how much that baby cost."

"Otis, you surprise me."

"I went to night school Got my diploma, too. Just 'cause I look like a slob don't mean I'm stupid. Don't mean I ain't watching what interests me. Kills the time."

"I'll bet you saw a lot more than you're copping to. I'm going to need you to sign a statement later." Smitty scowled, "Give it some thought, Mr. Grimes."

Otis smirked, "Anytime, Deputy, like I told you, I ain't going nowhere." He opened the drawer, took out his magazine, and put his feet back on the desk.

Smitty grimaced as he walked out of the office and trudged up the stairway to twenty six. He burned his hand on the railing. *Damn!* he snatched his hand away. *What idiot contractor would use metal railings in the desert?* He thought.

"Hey, Smitty. You get anything from the desk jockey?"

"Yeah. He's a perfect snitch. We could use a man with his talents. What's up Ernie?"

Ernie turned to Smitty, "I don't think this guy did himself, looks more like a homicide. Just a feeling right now, we'll know more after the autopsy. We're almost finished getting prints in here. Coroner should be here pretty soon. Name on the victim's driver's license is Earl Landers."

"Landers? That name rings a bell. Now where did I hear that name?" Smitty shook his head.

"Mitch, the motel clerk saw a man go up to twenty six. He ID'd Leonard Costa's car."

"That puts a twist on the case."

"I'm going over to room twenty three to question the lady with the tattoos."

Smitty knocked on the door. The number three had lost a screw and flipped over to look like a fancy 'E'. Tiny opened the door and smiled, her gold tooth flashed. "Hi, good looking. What can I do for yuh?"

It takes all kinds, Smitty thought. He showed his ID. "Ma'am, I need to ask you some questions."

"That's Ms. Tina Turner, no relation to the singer. Everybody calls me Tiny. Ask away!"

This lady's flying. Smells like she took a bath in whiskey, Smitty observed silently. "Ms. Turner, did you happen to see the two men in twenty six?"

"Met one of them a couple of days ago. Introduced myself. He didn't have any time for little Tiny though. Got the feeling he was more interested in guys. He brought one of his fancy friends up here this morning. The guy was generous though. Gave me a bottle of Jack Daniels before he left."

"Did you hear anything?"

"You bet, and when I saw him leaving today, I complained about the noise. Those guys had the TV turned up full blast. That's when he gave me the bottle of Jack. It was half empty, but I can't complain. Good booze!"

Tiny confirmed the description that the clerk had given. Said the man didn't tell her his name. She didn't have any more information about him or the dead man, but she willingly gave the empty Jack Daniels bottle to the deputy. Smitty thanked Tiny and went back to the crime scene.

Chapter 32

August 13, 1999
Marietta Ranch

Swirls of steam followed Carrie from the bathroom. She bounced onto the bed. "Sunny, I know it's getting late, but I can't sleep yet."

"I could read to you for a while." Sunny picked out a book of short stories from a built-in bookcase.

"Tell me one of Daniel's stories."

"Those aren't the best for bedtime."

"Please!" Carrie insisted.

I smiled and put the book back on the shelf. "Okay. I can't tell it the way Daniel does, but I'll give it a try." I snuggled next to Carrie and closed my eyes for a moment.

"Once, long ago at the beginning of things, there were twin brothers, Mukat and Tamaioit. They were always fighting about who was ..."

"Daniel has a twin. Do they fight?"

"I guess they don't get along too well. Anyway, there were two brothers and ..."

Carrie piped up, "They created the first people."

"Yes, but they couldn't see what they had done, so they created light. They blew the stars and then the sun from their mouths."

"And Tamaioit was in such a rush to make his people that they were ugly."

I nodded. "And the brothers continued to quarrel until Tamaioit left and took all he had created with him. He caused terrible earthquakes and other disasters that threatened to destroy Mukat's creations, but Mukat won and protected the people."

Carrie nodded wisely, "But Mukat wasn't all good. He gave poison fangs to Rattlesnake."

"Yes, and Rattlesnake killed one of the people and made them angry with him. Frog was chosen to spy on Mukat and witched him."

Carrie giggled. "Frog found out where Mukat went to the bathroom and," Carrie scrunched up her face, "Frog ate it. Yuck."

"Carrie, where did you hear that?"

"Daniel told me."

"Maybe you should be telling me this story."

"Oh, Sunny, please … I'll listen."

"So Mukat got sick and died, but before he did, he told the People to burn his body so that Coyote couldn't eat him. But Coyote came back just in time, grabbed Mukat's heart, blood streaming, and fled over the hills. And that's why you see red streaks on the mountains today."

"But Sunny, Daniel says Mukat's heart made Coyote sick. That's why coyotes are so skinny."

"Uh huh, but when hunting is good, the coyotes are fat. You've seen them when we go riding in the evenings here."

Carrie nodded. "Well, I guess … but could someone witch me like that?"

"No, Carrie, it's a myth; a way to explain how people came to be and there are many different versions of the story. I like mine the best. Now get into bed. You're going to have a big day tomorrow." I wondered what Daniel was thinking about, scaring Carrie like that. *She's just a little girl.*

I had just turned off the lights in the living room when there was a knock at the door. I was expecting Leon, but it was Daniel towering above me.

The security lights illuminated the black and white that brought Daniel back to the ranch, its hopped up engine sounded like the growl of an injured wolf as the car drove out of the gate.

In the shimmering twilight, I could almost imagine Daniel wearing the garments of an ancient medicine man as he whispered urgently, "Sunny, I feel a gathering of darkness. There are forces at work that wish to destroy us, but the main thrust right now is directed at you. Somehow it ties in with the Whitewater killer. When I saw the pictures today, I could feel your presence. I don't know how you're involved, but you're in danger."

Daniel's eyes were dilated; he seemed to be speaking from an unnatural source. "I had a warning. I don't know if we can change the events that I see. I told Mitch and Smitty that this had nothing to do with me, but I was wrong."

"You're frightening me," I shivered. "I think someone broke into the bunkhouse. Leon is checking it out now."

Daniel touched my cheek gently, but his fingers sent chills down my spine. I jerked back involuntarily. "Daniel?"

His broad shoulders were already disappearing between the dark and the stark glow of the security lights.

Far-fetched as Daniel's warning seemed at the time, I felt an urgency to check on Carrie. She slept peacefully on the fold out couch in the living room.

I tried to shake off the apprehension I felt, and checked the doors and windows to be sure they were locked. With her enigmatic eyes, Chowder followed every move I made. Shadow leaned against the couch, her giant head placed protectively on Carrie's arm.

I'm losing it, I thought. *I can't let this get to me.*

A few minutes later Daniel pounded on the door. Sunny peered through the spyhole and opened the door. "Daniel, what's wrong?"

"Call an ambulance! It's Leon. He's still breathing but someone hit him hard. I don't know how badly he's hurt. The phone line in the bunkhouse is cut. I'm going back to tend to Leon."

I called 911 and activated the automatic gate opener so the ambulance could get in. I told Shadow to guard Carrie, grabbed a flashlight, and went out, locking the door behind me. I ran over to the bunkhouse. That may have been one of the biggest mistakes of my life.

I found Daniel holding a folded, blood-soaked handkerchief to Leon's head. It seemed an eternity before I heard the ambulance siren. I could see the flashing lights at the gate. "Hurry, hurry!" Leon's eyes were closed, his face too chalky white even for a redhead.

A shadowy figure watched Sunny as she ran down to the bunkhouse. *Leon blew it. Now's the time.* The trailer door was easy. He slipped the lock quietly, only to meet the dog on alert. As Shadow leaped at his throat, he thrust the sharp tip of his knife into the dog's chest. Shadow's teeth met the attacker's hand and ripped the skin, but she was too hurt to do more. Carrie started to scream, but the chloroform-soaked rag covered her face. When her little form was still, the intruder picked her up in his arms; blood still dripping from his hand. He stayed in the dark shadows and walked quickly behind the trees where his vehicle was hidden.

He lay Carrie down on the seat and covered her with the flannel imitation Navajo blanket he used to protect the seat from the sun. He eased slowly away from the trees to the highway.

Damn dog! He thought; intent on the road. *Hurts like hell!* Scowling, he wrapped the still-bleeding hand with the red cleaning rag he kept on the dash. It took about twenty minutes to get to the house. "Good. Leon left the lights off," he muttered to himself. He pushed a button on the remote, waited for the garage door to open, and drove in. Checking at first that Carrie was well-hidden under the blanket and out cold, he hurried out the side door to the back yard. The door of the garden shed creaked on rusty metal hinges as he yanked it open. He paused briefly as he scanned the inside of the shed. With a satisfied smirk on his face, he walked confidently back to the garage, lifted Carrie, and carried her to the shed. Carrie was beginning to moan as he dumped her onto a camping cot that had been stored in a dusty corner. He quickly unrolled some duct tape, put a silver strip over Carrie's mouth, and wrapped more around her wrists and ankles.

"There, pretty girl. I'll see you in a few." He closed the plywood door, found the hook, and snapped it on the latch.

He lurched into the bathroom, washed his bleeding hand, poured antiseptic over the wound, and bandaged it. *Screw Leon, he'd asked for it. I told him to stay out of this, but no; he had to play hero again.*

Chapter 33

Marietta Ranch

Flashing emergency lights lent an eerie red and blue cast to the yellow security lights at the Marietta. Paramedics took over and put Leon on a stretcher. They loaded him into the ambulance and drove away, the siren wailing.

Two sheriff's patrol cars arrived just as the ambulance pulled out. I left Daniel to answer their questions and went back to the trailer to check on Carrie.

When I got to the steps, Shadow was lying just inside the open door. There was blood everywhere. "Carrie!" I ran into the living room. Carrie wasn't on the couch. Shadow tried to lift her head; her dark brown eyes begging my forgiveness. She'd done all she could, the wounds in her chest and shoulder were bleeding profusely.

Daniel and the two deputies crunched up the walk to the trailer. Daniel started to run when he saw me crouched over Shadow. He took a quick look at her and shook his head. "Where's Carrie?"

I looked up, holding a chloroform-soaked rag. "She's gone."

Chapter 34

August 1999
Twin Palms Sheriff's Station

Captain Jeff Newhouser was unmistakably troubled. He nervously moved the file on his desk from one side to the other. Smitty walked in, sat down in the chair across the desk from Jeff, took off his hat and hit it against his knee, freeing a small cloud of dust into the air. "Captain?"

"Smitty, did Ernie get anything off that pendant?"

"He found a small amount of the victim's blood on it. Couldn't get any prints though. I called the organizer of the Indian pow wow and got the name of a jeweler who had a booth there. Juan Lopez. He works in silver and semi-precious gems. Sells his handicraft at flea markets, art shows, anywhere he can make a buck. He said he makes six different designs of that particular pendant. Usually he puts them on a leather thong and sells them for ten dollars each. The toad design wasn't his. It was a special request. He didn't know who placed the order, or at least he wouldn't admit to it. He was paid in advance for two of them. He said he was given two envelopes and was told to give the envelopes and pendants to anyone who came to his booth and said, 'the coyote walks'.

"I don't buy all of his story though. I think he knows something more than he's telling, but he swears he just did what he was paid to do. He said that one of the security guards at the fiesta gave him the right message. The guy took the envelopes and the pendants. Didn't remember the face, just the uniform. He thinks it was a deputy working on his own time. He had a drawing of the pendant. He got a peculiar look on this face and asked me if I wanted it. Then he confessed that he'd looked into the envelopes. Claims he saw ten one-hundred dollar bills inside each one. Jeff, this is weird shit."

"Smitty, I'm going to ask Daniel about this. If we haven't totally alienated him, he might be willing to help us figure out what this is about." Jeff looked thoughtfully at Smitty. "Nobody around here mentioned anything about moonlighting at the fiesta, did they?"

Smitty replied defensively, "I haven't heard anything."

Jeff speculated further, "The money puts a different slant on this. It's too much for one night's security work. I was certain the murders were done by a lone serial killer, but that much money in the envelope makes me wonder if there isn't something else going on here."

"I know, Jeff. It seems like someone's trying to make it appear that the killer is a black magic weirdo. It's spooky, but I agree with you, there has to be more to it."

"Smitty, I want you to ask around. Don't scare anyone off. If it was one of our deputies there, we don't want him to get wise. I put a memo out requesting that all after-hours work be authorized. We better hope to God it wasn't one of our guys.

"I understand."

"I've got pressure coming down from the media, big time! We have to get a break on the Whitewater Canyon killings soon. This is beginning to look like a cult killing. People are frightened. Frightened people do dangerous things. We've already had an assault on an innocent citizen because his neighbor was sure he was the killer. We aren't looking too good right now."

Mitch Tolly came through the open door. "Captain, you wanted to see me?"

"Mitch, I want you to check something out. We know two of the missing girls had dome contact with this department prior to their abductions. I want you to check out the Wilson girl. See if there was any contact there."

"What are you thinking, Jeff?"

"I'm not sure. Just check it out."

"Yes, sir." Mitch didn't like this assignment, but Jeff was his boss. He went back to the desk and was surprised to see Sergeant Neely. "Hey Neely, aren't you usually working burglary? Where's Jerry?"

"He took a few days off and Diaz called in sick. I'm just filling in. I got called back form my vacation. I said I'd work if they needed me. The extra pay always helps. Anything I can help you with?"

"Yeah, check to see if Jennet Wilson, the first Whitewater victim, had any contact with this department. It doesn't have to be an arrest, she was only 11 years old, and I don't remember anything said about her being in trouble."

"Sure, I'll check it out. What's up?"

"Not sure. Jeff has a burr up his ass."

Ernie Wood walked past the desk on his way to the Captain's office. "Hi Mitch. How's it going?"

"Ernie, this Whitewater Canyon case is in trouble."

"Yeah, I have to see the Captain. He called me in for a report. Seems the media are really coming down on the department. He wants to get a report to the press, one that shows some progress on the case."

"Neely, why are you on the desk today?"

"Um, well, Diaz is out again and Branson has the day off."

Ernie grinned and shook his head. "From what I hear, Diaz is working on getting a permanent vacation. His moonlighting as private security is getting in the way of his job here."

Neely looked thoughtful for a minute, "You know, Ernie, Diaz mentioned something about security work on the Rez. Was he down there at the pow wow?"

"I don't know. I heard the Captain was asking about that. Wasn't there something about asking permission to work off hours?"

"Yeah, we all got a memo about it."

"Scuttlebutt has it that Diaz liberated a couple of shotguns from that load of weapons that we destroyed last month. Just a rumor, no proof. If he ever gets caught, that's one ignoramus out there."

Neely tapped his pen on the desk. "No loss. Never did like that guy, there's something really fishy about him. He offered to sell me a genuine Indian olla for almost nothing. I should have told Jeff, but you know ... Anyway, I hear he got transferred down here because he got into some kind of trouble. He's an arrogant SOB; makes Branson look like a prince."

"Well, I don't have much use for Branson, either. What an irritating little wimp. He ought to work for the IRS," Mitch sniggered.

Not to be outdone, Ernie quipped, "Nope, maybe at a pizza parlor. He could grate the cheese." Ernie chuckled to himself as he walked into Jeff Newhouser's office.

"Jeff, you wanted to see me?"

"Yeah, what do you have on the Whitewater Canyon case?"

Ernie opened a large manila folder and put it on the gray metal desk. Jeff kept his desk immaculate; the in and out trays were both empty. His medal of valor was framed conservatively and hung on the wall next to several other awards and commendations. The only softness in the room was an eleven by fourteen photograph of his wife and three children centered on the top shelf of a cherry-wood bookcase that housed his law enforcement books.

"Jeff, everything we have is right there: photographs, reports, evidence, and statements. We just got a report back on the hair found on the sheet wrapped around the Wilson girl. Came from a long-haired cat. There were some spots of cat blood on it too. The pendant the posse turned up had a small splatter of the victim's blood on it. No fingerprints. The shovel had blood from two of the victims on the handle, but nothing on the blade. We still need a murder weapon. Couldn't get any usable fingerprints. The MO is the same for all victims. I'm ninety-nine percent sure that the killings were all done by the same perp. We found several short black hairs on each of the victims. Probably pubic hair. They're a match. You get a suspect and we'll put him away. One more thing, I heard that Diaz could be the deputy who picked up the silver pendants at the fiesta."

"Thanks, Ernie. I'll talk to Diaz. Would you ask Sergeant Neely to bring me a display board? I need to get a better overall picture of what we have here."

"You bet. Wish I had more for you."

"Me too, Ernie. Me too." Jeff Newhouser was definitely a man carrying a heavy burden. His tired eyes revealed he was barely surviving the constant pressure from this case. He glanced at the photo of his wife and their three daughters. "Thanks Ernie." Jeff said it as a dismissal, not from gratitude.

Chapter 35

August 13, 1999
Marietta Ranch

I knew I'd blown it big time. Yellow crime scene tape flapped loosely around the trailer. Carrie was missing or worse. Leon was in surgery at the hospital getting stitches in his scalp. Shadow lay whimpering in the back of the Toyota, her wounds seeping blood through the bandages. Chowder was in hiding somewhere on the ranch. She wasn't in the trailer.

I drove like a mad woman to the emergency animal hospital. I still had to go down to the station to answer more questions about what happened, and I hadn't talked to Caroline and Lenny yet. If it hadn't been for Rick, I would still be at the ranch answering questions. I should have been with Carrie. *Damn! I should have stayed.*

Laura Kingston, the vet who took care of the horses at the ranch, was on duty at the emergency clinic. She volunteers several days a month with the smaller critters so even animals that belong to people without much money can have the necessary care. In her late twenties, she looks more like a blonde cheerleader than one of the best large animal vets in the county. She took Shadow into her surgery.

In despair, I sat in the waiting room for about thirty minutes trying not to think. Guilt, like a lead weight, pulled my spirits down. Uselessly I kept going over and over what had happened. Something was nagging at me and I just couldn't put my finger on it. When Laura came out from the back, she smiled, "Sunny, I think Shadow's going to be all right. As far as I can tell, nothing vital was cut. She lost a lot of blood, but I patched her up and have an IV running. She can go home in a couple of days. How did it happen? It looks like a knife wound."

"Laura, I can't talk about it now. Thanks for pulling Shadow through." I left the vet hospital and drove over to Desert Dune Hospital. As I walked in Rick met me at the desk.

Chapter 36

August 13, 1999
Desert Dunes Hospital

"Hi Sunshine. Good news! Leon's conscious, out of recovery and in room 102. He'll live, but they don't know if he'll remember what happened. The crime lab's testing the blood samples and getting finger prints from your trailer. Do you have a place to stay tonight?"

"Rick, I have to get back to the ranch."

"Look, Sunshine, your place is a mess."

Sometimes I bite off more than I can chew. I can't seem to admit I need help, especially if I do. I tossed a quick smile at Rick. "I'm going to have to clean it up sometime. I'll camp out in the main house. Has anyone contacted the Costas?" I dreaded facing them. *Mea culpa, mea maxima culpa,* echoed in my brain.

"Sergeant Neely already contacted Caroline. He sent a deputy over to talk with the Costas. Sunshine, I know you feel this is your fault, but it isn't. You could have been lying dead beside Shadow. Whoever kidnapped Carrie probably would have killed you if you'd been there. You're good with a gun, but if someone wants to get you badly enough, they will."

"I know that, Rick, but Carrie was my responsibility. I should have stayed with her. It should have been me."

"Stop it! That's nonsense. We'll find Carrie." Rick put his arm protectively around me. "You watch out for yourself, Sunny. Who knew Carrie was at your place?"

"As far as I know it was just you and the Costas." I thought a minute. "Of course, Leon and Daniel knew, but Leon's here in the hospital and Daniel didn't get back until Leon had already gone to check on the bunkhouse."

"Remember those hang-up calls you were getting?"

"Yeah, I had caller ID installed, but there haven't been any more."

"I was just thinking. Maybe ..." Rick paused. "When did those calls start?"

"Rick, I don't remember exactly, but I guess it was about a year after Johnny died when I got the first one, then every once in a while since then; never often enough for me to get worried though. I just chalked it up to kids playing pranks or a wrong number or something. I don't even know if it's one person doing it."

Chapter 37

August 14, 1999
Marietta Ranch

Cumulus clouds were suspended over the Orocopia Mountains and promised to unleash a summer thunderstorm. The air was so heavy with humidity I could almost hold it in my hands. It draped like a dismal damp scarf around my shoulders. I yearned for a deluge to wash away my foul mood.

Ernie's mobile forensic unit was still parked in front of the bunkhouse. Daniel walked over to the car. "Sunny, there's nothing you can do here right now. I'm going over to the hospital to see Leon. He's asked to talk to me. You want to come?"

"I just came from there. I don't want to go back, not even for Leon."

Daniel's concern for me was obvious. A compulsion to weep nearly overwhelmed me. I couldn't go into the trailer yet; I felt violated and dispossessed. "You're right about one thing though, I need to do something. I feel so helpless. Carrie's in danger because of me. Tell Leon I'm glad he's doing better. I'll go over to his place and make sure that Bubbles and Squeak are all right." Leon had two large cats with pointy ears and bobbed tails; the result of an unlikely union between a domestic tabby and a wild cat. We'd found the mother dead and Leon had hand-raised the two kittens.

"Sunny, don't blame yourself."

"I shouldn't have left her alone, Daniel."

"What is done is done. You could not have prevented this any more than a pebble can withstand a flash flood. Coyote, the trickster, has his paws in this. Appearances can be deceiving. Where Coyote roams, Antonio isn't far away. I keep thinking about that amulet. The toad is used as a death curse. We found it carved on Mary's door. Those amulets must have something to do with what happened to Mary, too.

"I don't see how one of them turned up near the body of that little girl. I don't know how Carrie is involved. Sunny, this does threaten you both. The threads of madness and hatred and greed are so tangled that I can't see clearly."

"No! Daniel, you don't think that monster has Carrie, do you?"

Daniel's expression was as unreadable as a stone. "I don't know. Last night an owl followed me home. It was a warning. An evil darkness is pursuing us; this isn't over yet." Daniel put his hand on my shoulder. "Sunny, be careful. There's more trouble coming. Watch your back. I wish you were coming with me."

Chapter 38

Desert Dunes Hospital

Daniel walked quietly into Leon's room at the hospital. He watched for a while until Leon opened his eyes. "Leon, you asked for me?"

Leon sat up putting his hands to the bandages on his head. "Daniel, I really made a mess of this. I didn't know Sunny and Carrie would be harmed."

"I believe you. Don't blame yourself."

"Is Carrie okay?"

"She will be … I'm almost certain of that."

"I think I know who's behind this." Leon shook his head sadly. "I met Greg Hanson shortly after I immigrated to the states. His family had a ranch in Las Vegas where they kept a stable of race horses. I'd been a damn good trainer in England and the owners I worked for suggested I see the Hanson's when I got over here. Greg's dad took one look at my recommendations and offered me a job. The problem was there was a lot of blue sky in my references." Leon suddenly got pale and lay back on the pillow.

In his mind Daniel heard the sound of horses' hooves pounding, felt the green foggy morning; a vision suddenly turned upside down, the horse struggling, screaming. Leon was screaming.

"Leon, we've been friends a long time, I know you wouldn't hurt Sunny or Carrie. You don't have to tell me all this."

"No, I'm all right. I need to tell someone."

Leon continued, his voice barely above a whisper, "Before I left England, one of the horses I was training reared over backward with me. I didn't get out of the way fast enough. Just about every bone in my body was fractured or crushed. Rehabilitation was a long, painful process. I got hooked on the medications I was taking for pain. When the doctors wouldn't prescribe the meds anymore, I got them illegally. I was still using when I started working for the Hanson's.

"Mr. Hanson told me Greg had gotten into some trouble in the service. He'd been kicked out with a dishonorable discharge. If it hadn't been for his parents' money and some fancy dancing lawyers, Greg would've landed in prison. Well, poor little rich boy ended up running the horse ranch and was well on his way to running it into the ground. He was gambling heavily and owed the wrong people too much money. He'd sold off the best stock and I was supposed to pull off some kind of miracle with what was left.

"Greg wasn't a user, but he'd gotten into dealing drugs big time to pay off his debts. It didn't take him long to figure out I had a problem. He got me my drugs, and I covered for him with his family.

"One night, I heard screaming in one of the stalls. I found Greg attempting to rape the thirteen year old daughter of one of the ranch hands. He was beating her with his fists and ripping her clothes. I pulled him off the girl and she ran to her father. I tried to talk them out of it, but they pressed charges and I had to testify or be arrested on drug charges. This time Greg went to prison; his parents disowned him. I went to drug rehab. I've been clean ever since."

Leon paused for a minute, catching his breath. "Greg got an early release, found out where I was living, and paid me an unwelcome visit. He threatened to tell the owners of Marietta Ranch about my past if I didn't let him use my place when he was in town. He even sent me a telegram telling me I was fired. He laughed about it, but I got the message.

"He told me he went to college with Sunny and her friend Caroline. Then he started asking questions about what they were doing now; acted like he was a friend of theirs. I stupidly let it slip that Carrie was staying with Sunny. God, I feel terrible about it now. Greg is a malicious, evil man.

"When I figured out that someone was hiding out in the bunkhouse, I was sure it was Greg. I didn't know what he was up to, but I knew it wasn't good. When I opened the door somebody hit me. Next thing I know, I wake up here. I didn't remember anything about what happened at first."

"Did you see him, Leon?"

Leon shook his head, "No, but who else could it have been?"

"You're going to have to tell the authorities, Leon."

"I know, Daniel."

"There's a deputy outside."

"Will you ask him to come in?"

"Yes."

Daniel opened the door and spoke to the man sitting by the door. "Deputy, Mr. MacIntyre wants to talk to you."

Chapter 39

August 14, 1999
Marietta Ranch

Chowder still hadn't shown up. I'd spent most of the morning down at the department answering questions. Ernie and the crime lab guys were finishing up their investigation. We were no closer to finding Carrie than we had been last night. I called the hospital from the main house. Leon was out of his room.

Driving out to Leon's, I tried to get a handle on what happened last night. Leon had been very nervous yesterday, as if there was something he wanted to tell me. He was obviously relieved when Carrie showed up, but still tense about something.

The Whitewater Canyon killer had already claimed three victims and Daniel seemed to think the killer was tied in somehow with Carrie and me. Daniel's visions of 'evil' and 'darkness', forces out to destroy us, frighten me. I knew Daniel's mystical side well enough to believe him. Some malignant force was propelling me and the people I care about toward a vortex of disaster.

My subconscious must have been driving the car, because suddenly there was Leon's house just up the block. I saw a black car pulling into his driveway. The garage door opened and the car went inside. *Now, who is that?* I wondered, *Maybe a friend of Leon's going over to help out while he's in the hospital.* I pulled up in front of the garage, got out, went to the front door, and pushed the doorbell. Nobody answered so I went through the side gate to the back of the house where Leon grew his vegetables and herbs. The door to the garden shed was open.

"Hello, anybody there?" I poked my head around the corner. I should have listened to Daniel. The last thing I remember was a whooshing sound, a burst of pain in my head, then nothing.

When I opened my eyes, pain shattered my thoughts; I couldn't see. *I'm blind!* I thought. *God, what happened?* I could hear someone moving nearby, and a muffled sound of a voice. It took me a few moments to realize that it was night, and that I wasn't blinded, but warm, sticky liquid was dripping down my face. I tasted my own blood. I heard something nearby thrashing about; someone was in the shed with me.

"Hmmee, hmmmeee," the sounds were frantic. I scooted carefully toward them, trying to see where they were coming from. Little hammers in my head were pounding, trying to get out. I blindly stretched out my arm and felt a bed of some kind, a camp cot. I could feel the canvas. Someone was moving awkwardly from side to side. My eyes slowly adjusted to a dim light coming through the wooden slats. A neighbor behind Leon's house must have turned on his porch light.

I could barely see a face with some kind of tape across the mouth. I ripped it off quickly. "Sunny! Oh Sunny, you found me!"

It was Carrie.

"He tied my hands and feet. I thought he was going to kill me when he came back, then I saw you. He hit you awful hard. You fell. There was blood all over your head. He told me you were dead and if I didn't behave, I would be, too. He's coming back Sunny. We have to get out of here!"

I ripped the rest of the tape off her wrists and ankles. The shed door was locked. I looked around in the dim light and found a pry bar. I remembered reading that, if you have a lever and a place to stand, you can move the earth. The shed door was pretty flimsy and it didn't take long to break the hinges off the door. I was reeling, a sound like a hive of bees swarmed in my head. Somehow the two of us got out to where I'd left the car. A streetlight down the block cast a dim glow. The garage door was still open, but the car was gone.

My Toyota was still parked in the driveway. All I could think of was escape until I opened the car door. That pond scum had taken my keys!

"Carrie, crawl behind that bush and stay there! Don't make a sound no matter what happens!"

She nodded.

Barely able to keep my balance, I staggered like a drunk up the walkway to the house next door. Sounds of a popular television cop show were blaring and blue light was flashing through the blinds. I banged on the front door. The porch light illuminated the shape of a middle-aged man with his belly hanging out over his shorts standing in the doorway with the sound of police sirens screaming behind him. He held a can of beer in his hand. I was afraid he would slam the door in my face.

"You have to help me! Call 911. Someone tried to kill me. Please help!"

I must have looked like a victim from his TV show, but the guy pulled me inside, sat me down on a kitchen chair, and told me he had been trained in first aid. He asked me if I wanted him to help me. I nearly screamed, "Yes!" He did a quick assessment of my condition and called 911. Once I heard him place the call, I felt that I could trust him. I had said those same words to victims so many times. Now I was the one in need of assistance. I staggered back to the door and called for Carrie to come out of her hiding place. She slowly stood up and started to sob.

"Carrie, it's okay."

The man took her by the hand and led her into the kitchen.

"Your little girl is fine, just shaken up. You need medical treatment. An ambulance and the police are on the way." He made a pressure bandage from a kitchen towel and told me to press it against the side of my head. It turned out our rescuer was a volunteer fireman.

"Can you answer some questions?"

I managed to look up; it was a Palm Springs Police Officer. I was never so glad to see a city cop. I'd had a couple of run-ins with the PSPD. The speeding tickets had been expensive, but as of this minute, all was forgiven.

I explained who I was and that Carrie had been kidnapped by the man who had nearly killed me and that he might be coming back. I gave him a description of the car and told him I thought Greg Hanson was responsible. He radioed his headquarters to put out an all-points bulletin and asked for a couple of their officers to stake out Leon's house. I asked him to contact the Sheriff's Department and talk to Deputy Rick Tower, gave him Caroline's phone number, and asked him to call the Costas and let them know Carrie was safe. Suddenly the day was definitely over for me. My head felt like it was about to detach from my body and I passed out in the arms of the PSPD officer without even asking if he was married. The ambulance arrived and took Carrie and me to Desert Dunes Hospital.

Caroline and Lenny met us just as we were being rolled through the emergency room entrance. I looked around for Rick but he wasn't there. After the doctor checked Carrie, and the officers took her statement, she was allowed to go home with her parents. Caroline stopped by to make sure I was all right, but she was in such a rush to get Carrie home. I was determined to leave with her, but the ER doctors weren't having any of it. I had to stay the night for observation. They'd give me back my freedom the next day if all systems were functioning in accordance with 'AMA' doctor-approved standards.

God, I hate hospitals, was my last thought before the lights went out again, but this time I was in a hospital bed with all the trimmings: barf basin, bedpan, empty water pitcher, call light somewhere under the tightly wrapped sheets, and an IV dripping some unknown fluid in my arm.

"I want my clothes, and I want them now!"

The nurse bustled in and turned on the light over my bed, just as I was about to pull out the IV.

"Busted! I can't seem to do anything right." I grinned guiltily up at the figure dressed in hospital white.

"Ah ah ah!" She scolded. "Be good now. You lost a lot of blood. It won't hurt you to stick it out a little longer. You thirsty? Let me fill the pitcher for you. You need a little rest and by tomorrow you should be able to go home."

"Madge?" My nurse was Jerry Branson's sister.

I was thirsty and utterly exhausted. A wave of pain went through me and I lay back down on the bed. Madge was all 'nurse', not exactly friendly; but she wasn't cold and aloof the way she'd been the night Jerry and I had dinner at their house. Maybe I could find out why she'd been so upset with us. I can't seem to keep my nose out of other people's business.

"Okay, I give up. I'll be good, Madge. Nice to see you again, but I wish we were somewhere else."

Madge lost her smile, "Sunny, I have to talk to you. I don't have time right now. I'll stop by in the morning before I go home." She brought the ice water, explained how all the buttons worked, and turned off the main light. "Good night, Sunny. I'll be checking on you. You're going to be fine; a little bruised and swollen, but not too much worse for the wear. Your head is going to hurt for a while and your shoulder is badly bruised. You're lucky the collar bone wasn't broken. Be back in a couple of hours. Good night."

As I drifted into sleep I wondered what on earth Madge wanted to talk to me about. When I first met her she'd acted like a real snob. Something was bothering her.

The next thing I knew, there was Madge in her starched white uniform gently shaking me. "Wake up. I'm going to ask you some questions. "What is your name?"

"You have to be kidding. You woke me up to find out my name? You know who I am."

"You have a possible concussion and I'm just checking to make sure you're all right."

The questions may have seemed silly to me, but they told her if anything was wrong. She took my temperature, blood pressure, and checked my reflexes.

"I know it seems dumb, but it's necessary."

I remembered my first aid training. "Okay," I grumbled, "My name is Sunny Morgan. I live on the Marietta Ranch. Today is Saturday, August the 14th, 1999. I was hit on the head and I'm in Desert Dunes Hospital. Anything else?"

"Who's President of the United States?"

I teased, "Oh God, it's not Nixon, is it?" I didn't even get a smile.

I guess I must have passed the test, because Madge walked out after writing a few things down in my chart. My head hurt, and my right arm was wrapped against my chest. It seems the blow glanced off my head and nearly fractured my collar bone. The doctor came in. He commented that, if whatever hit me had landed on my head full force, I wouldn't be here to complain, so count my blessings.

"Right!" I complained, "How perspicacious of you."

"No need to talk dirty now." The doctor went away, laughing to himself.

"Gotcha, doc."

The compulsion to use four-letter words often gives way to my love of language. Forget Playgirl magazine; I keep a dictionary on the shelf in the bathroom. I wonder what Freud would say about that? Anyway, it's not what the words mean, but the expression on your face when you say them.

The next time Madge came in, I was awake and my head was pounding. I knew she couldn't give me anything for the pain, but maybe she could satisfy my curiosity. "Madge, what did you want to talk to me about?"

She was busy straightening the bed, not looking at me, "Jerry started acting peculiar after you stopped seeing him. Sunny, did he have anything to do with this?"

"Madge, what do you mean?"

She avoided answering me directly. "Jerry seems troubled and I think it has something to do with the two of you."

"I can't imagine why. But now that you brought it up, I wondered why you wouldn't talk to me the night we had dinner at your place. You acted like Jerry didn't have a right to be there in his own home."

She looked at me in surprise. "Jerry doesn't live with me; he has a place up in Yucca Valley." Madge paused a moment, grimaced, and then as though she was giving up a family secret, continued, "Jerry called me from the theater about an hour before you showed up and ordered me to fix dinner for you. I'd had it up to here." She put her hand over her head.

"It wasn't that I didn't want to get to know you." She shook her head and attempted to smile. "Jerry's always pulling mind games on me, and I don't like it. Something's going on with him and I thought you might know what it is. You're the first woman he's shown any interest in for a long time. I thought it might have been my fault that you stopped seeing him."

"Madge, I'm not ready to get into a relationship right now. Besides I don't really think Jerry and I have enough in common to even try. The night we had dinner at your house I tried to explain that to him, but he didn't want to listen." I didn't describe to Madge the evening when Jerry kept trying to kiss me; or that when I pushed him away he left, slamming the door behind him. "I was surprised when he asked me out again. I told him no and I wasn't too nice about it. He's treated me like something the cat dragged in ever since. What made you think he might have hurt me?"

"I'm sorry, Sunny. He doesn't take rejection very well." Her small mouth tightened up even more and what little warmth had been in her eyes was gone.

A different nurse woke me up two hours later. When I asked about Madge, she said that Madge finished her shift and went home. In the morning, the doctors agreed to let me go home as long as I had someone who could drive me. I was about to call Caroline when Rick showed up.

"Hi Sunshine." He kissed my brow lightly. "I would have been here sooner, but you really started something last night. We're trying to find the guy who grabbed Carrie and attacked you. I'll tell you all about it on the way to your place. Daniel says your trailer is cleaned up. Chowder showed up after the maintenance crew left. Laura called and said Shadow is still weak and she's going to have to have more surgery, but not to worry. She's holding her own. Every time a car drives up the road to the ranch, Max hangs his head over the fence looking for you."

"So let's go! A person could die in here!"

Rick laughed, "Sunshine, you got it! Take my arm."

Hospital policies really irritate me. I was ready to walk out the door when the day shift nurse insisted that I leave in a wheelchair. "Insurance," she pronounced.

Grumbling, I sat.

The chair was labeled *3 North* but I'd been on the second floor. Made me wonder who'd been in it before me. I briefly experienced a perverse satisfaction that even wheelchairs could get high jacked.

She pushed me out to the curb where Rick had parked his truck with the door open. I got out of the wheelchair, took my bundle of hospital memorabilia, and tossed it gleefully into a trash barrel near the entrance. I was exhilarated. "Free at last!"

Rick glanced over at me like I'd lost my mind. "Sunny get in the truck! Let's get you home before they come out with the butterfly nets."

Chapter 40

August 15, 1999

We were making the wide turn out of Rancho Mirage into Palm Desert when Rich turned to me, "No matter what you think about Jerry Branson, he's pretty good at putting together composites of suspects from what witnesses remember. He wants you and Carrie to come down to help him put together on of the guy who attacked you."

"Rick, I didn't even see who clobbered me. I stuck my head in the door and that was all I remember until I came to and found Carrie in the shed with her mouth taped. I don't even know if Carrie can identify her kidnapper or not, but it's worth a try. Speaking of getting clobbered, is Leon still in the hospital?"

"The doctors are going to keep him for another few days. He walked down the hallway on his own today. Looks like he's going to be fine. He still has some questions to answer about why the kidnapper used his place to hide Carrie. Does the name Handy Miller sound familiar?"

"No, never heard of him."

"How about Greg Harwin?"

"No."

"It looks like Leon is involved in this somehow."

"I can't believe that. Leon would never hurt Carrie or me."

"One or maybe two men were staying at Leon's place. We got a warrant to search. There was a suitcase with a couple of hundred dollars in cash, a driver's license for a Handy Miller and a social security card for Greg Harwin in the guest bathroom. I'm going to see if the Costas can identify the picture on the license." Rick chuckled, "If everybody looked like their license pictures, the world would be full of really ugly people."

"Real funny, Rick."

"Sunshine, sometimes you have to laugh so you don't scream. Know what I mean? It's like a dead end with this investigation right now."

He paused and got a serious expression on his face, as if he were reluctant to continue. "Something's been bothering me about Leonard Costa. His name keeps coming up in another investigation. I know he's a friend of yours Sunny, but he was seen leaving the scene of a murder."

"Rick, I know there's an explanation for all of this. Lenny and Leon couldn't be involved in kidnapping and murder."

"I hope Leon can explain why the suspects were staying at his house. You know I've always liked Leon, but you nearly checked out permanently. There's a possibility he had something to do with it. What do you really know about Leon? Has he ever told you anything about his past?"

"Well, no." I had a lot to think about.

Rick dropped me off at the trailer. After I got out of the truck, he called me back.

"Sunshine, everything's cleaned up. Need anything?"

"Yeah, I'll grab my stuff and maybe you could take a look around inside. I'd feel better if I knew there weren't any bad guys in the closet."

"You got it."

I unlocked the door to the trailer and went inside and turned on all the lights while Rick checked out the trailer. "Rick, will you talk to Leon? I'm sure he's as much a victim as Carrie and I are. He wouldn't do anything to put us in danger. There has to be an explanation."

"I hope you're right," Rick sounded unconvinced. "Trailer's clean. No bad guys."

"Damn it, Rick. I can't believe Leon had anything to do with any of this. He showed me the ropes of managing a horse ranch, not the paperwork end, but the real stuff. Let me help deliver the foals, taught me to whisper in the ears of unruly colts and how to clean and trim the horses' hooves.

"Leon never talks about breaking a horse; he uses his voice and his hands to gentle an animal without destroying its spirit. I'll never believe that Leon could be responsible for hurting Carrie or me."

"Sunny, sometimes it's hard to figure why people do the things they do."

"But he treated me like a kid sister. He let Carrie and I tag along on his photography expeditions. He loves the desert and the birds and animals."

"You told me yourself that Leon doesn't like people very much."

"But he wouldn't hurt anyone."

Rick gave me a hug. I lay my head against his chest. For a second I thought he was going to kiss me, but he didn't. I wasn't sure if I was sorry or relieved.

"Okay, Sunshine, I'll do what I can. I'll check back with you later. Get some rest. You've had a hard couple of days. Lock your door."

"Um, okay." I felt as though I'd just missed the last bus home.

Shaking my head, I watched Rick propel down the road, dust and gravel flying. "I am going to have to post a speed limit sign." I said to no one in particular.

After Rick left, Chowder ran up to me and rubbed her soft orange fur against my legs, nearly tripping me as I bent over to stroke her with my one good hand. I forgot to ask Rick if the Toyota could be towed to the ranch, not that I could drive it until I had another key made. I was stuck here. "That may not be a bad thing," I muttered wearily.

I was tired and emotionally drained. Now that I knew Carrie was safe, I could rest. I was impatient to see Max and let him know he hadn't been abandoned, but first I needed to put in a meaningful connection with Chowder. Food. It was time to get an electric can opener. I managed to open the last can of tuna the old fashioned way and gave a few choice tidbits to Chowder. She nibbled at it and then sat staring at me. It was going to take more than tuna to make her forgive me this time.

There was no trace of blood in the trailer, but I knew it was still there even though I couldn't see it. No amount of scrubbing would make it go away. I'd get the painters in as soon as I could. Even then the memory would be there forever. At least the ugly sofa bed was gone; I didn't like it anyway.

Carrie was safe and Shadow would be home tomorrow. I took a deep breath, found a couple of withered carrots in the refrigerator, and went out to make amends with Max. I ducked under the fence and whistled. Max nickered joyfully, galloped over and nuzzled me. "Hey boy. Easy, big guy." I gave him the carrots, some big one-armed hugs, and went back to the trailer. I scolded Chowder, "At least Max is glad to see me."

It must have been Greg. I thought I had it figured out. When Caroline refused to give the money to Greg Hanson, he snatched Carrie. But maybe it wasn't Greg. I didn't see who hit me. Who was Handy Miller or Greg Harwin? Too many Gregs. It could be an alias.

I still didn't have a clue how Leon figured in this, but it was his place where Carrie had been hidden. Rick said that the Whitewater killer had to have had a place to keep his victims for a few days. What if somehow he used Leon's place without Leon knowing? Daniel didn't have a clear picture but he felt there was some connection between what was happening now and Mary's murder. And what was the connection with a pendant and a death curse? Three young girls. It was too much for my aching head. I decided a good night's sleep in my own bed was the best medicine; that, and a couple of Seconal. I'd face the world later.

Somewhere in the midst of swirling gold hats dripping with blood and blue ribbons wrapped tightly around my neck, I heard the phone ring, but the sound mixed in with my nightmare.

When I finally realized what the ringing was, the answering machine had already picked up with its cheery 'Leave a message at the beep'. I was so groggy that, by the time I got to the phone, whoever called was gone. I pushed the message button. Nothing but breathing. Someone was there. But he didn't say anything. *Here we go again*, I groaned, *but this time you aren't getting away with it*. I checked the caller ID. The number was familiar, I knew the number, but I couldn't place it. I knew I should wait for Rick to trace it, but I decided to dial the number anyway. I'd find out who'd been harassing me. I let it ring ten times but no answer and no machine. *I'll get you yet!* I went back to my bedroom and fell asleep with Chowder curled up around my bandaged head.

Chapter 41

August 1999
Twin Palms Sheriff Station

Deputy Tolly looked at his notes as he reported to Jeff Newhouser. "We ran Earl Landers' name through DMV. He's the owner of the truck that Tobias Black drove in the CHP shooting."

"How does Landers fit in with the shooting?"

"Jeff, we're questioning Black about him right now. Should know something soon."

"The autopsy showed that Earl Landers' blood alcohol level was so high, it's unlikely he was even conscious when he died. The coroner's ninety-nine percent sure the guy was murdered."

"Ernie said the same thing and he's usually right. Anything else?"

"Ernie got some good prints from the motel room. One set matched the maid, Theresa Picenzo. She cleaned the room that morning. There were a lot of partials, but in a motel room, who knows how many people have been in and out. The maid didn't do more cleaning than she had to. A couple of the prints matched the victim."

"Anything that could give us a lead?"

"There were some prints on a plastic cup we pulled out of the trash that we haven't gotten a match on yet. They aren't the victims or Costa's"

"What's going on with that?"

"Smitty and I are going to the Costa residence to question Leonard Costa. His Mercedes was seen at the motel around the time Landers was killed."

"Mitch, there could be a connection between this murder and Carrie Costa's kidnapping. Check it out."

"You got it, Captain." Mitch closed his small spiral notebook and put it in his back pocket.

Chapter 42

August, 1999
Marietta Ranch

I spent the next week catching up on the book work at the ranch, bored and frustrated. It was better than thinking about what had happened. Friday around four o'clock in the afternoon, the phone rang. This time I got it before the answering machine could pick up.

"Sunny, this is Brad. We just got a report of a missing girl up near Morongo Valley. San Bernardino Search and Rescue have asked us for mounted assistance. You feeling up to going?"

"Sure, if someone can pick me up. I can't ride, but I'll help you at CP."

"Rick was sure you'd want to go. He said to tell you he'd be over in about a half hour."

"Thanks Brad. I'll be ready." I knew I needed to do this.

"Sunny, you gotta get back on the horse, so to speak." Brad's a sweet man, but sometimes his little homilies are a bit much.

Rick drove up with his truck and horse trailer. I didn't want to look like an invalid, so I unwrapped my bandages and took my arm out of the sling. It was still a little tender but I felt almost human again. I got in the truck with Rick. Max nickered plaintively as we pulled out of the driveway. He wanted to go, too.

After we'd gone a couple of miles, I asked, "Rick, have they found out anything more about the man who kidnapped Carrie and attacked me?"

"Yep. You two were lucky. We don't have the DNA results from the blood samples, but we know the perp got a major dog bite. Shadow really got him before he stabbed her. He went to the ER and had the wound stitched up. I guess he didn't know that dog bites have to be reported.

"He signed his name as Handy Miller, the same name as we found on the driver's license at Leon's place. He claimed that it was his own dog that bit him. We're waiting for a report from CCI on the fingerprints we lifted from your trailer and Leon's place. We'll get him. We don't have anything on Greg Harwin yet, but from what we've found out, Miller is a nasty player. He ran a drug operation up in Pinyon. We've got one of his partners in jail right now ready to testify against him." Rick rolled his eyes in exasperation. "All we have to do is find Miller."

"Umm. A problem?"

"Yep. Miller doesn't have any history that we can find. That's not all that's maddening. Ernie says this guy's prints match some that we lifted at a murder scene."

"I guess I was lucky."

"Yes, you were, Sunshine." Rick had a peculiar look on his face, kind of like he'd just swallowed something nasty. "Something's come up. I need to ask you some questions about Leonard Costa. He was seen coming out of a murder victim's motel room. The room had been rented by a John Smith, but we found Handy Miller's prints there. There's evidence that leads back to Carrie's kidnapping and the attack on you. Why would Leonard Costa be at the motel even before Carrie was kidnapped? Do you know anything about it?"

"Lenny? No I can't imagine. Has anyone talked to Lenny? This guy they arrested, do you think he's the one who tried to kill Leon? Maybe there was more than one. Could someone else have been there and kidnapped Carrie?" I was thinking fast.

"Whoa! We arrested a guy named Tobias Black before Carrie was kidnapped. He may have something to do with the kidnapper, but he was in jail at the time when that happened. Mitch is going to talk with the Costas. We think that Carrie's kidnapping may be linked somehow to the motel murder.

"We're sure the man who attacked Leon is the same one who kidnapped Carrie and knocked you on the head, but we still need Leon's help to prove it. Leon's not cooperating. Says he doesn't remember anything, but I have a difficult time believing that. I think he knows something and he's not talking. He's pulling a fast one."

"That doesn't sound like the Leon I know. Rick, I ..."

Rick cut me off. "Don't worry about it Sunshine, I'm sure we'll be able to convince him to explain things."

I was going to tell Rick about Greg Hanson. I was almost certain that he and this Handy Miller were either the same person or working together. Suddenly, a semi with a double trailer cut in front of Rick's truck and nearly ran us off the road. In the few seconds it took Rick to get us straightened out, I decided I'd better talk with Caroline and Lenny before I said anything more. What could Lenny have to do with a murder? That decision nearly cost me my life.

I should have given Rick the phone number of the crank caller, too, but I was focused on trying to figure out how Greg Hanson fit into the picture. I know it's not much of an excuse, but a crank caller didn't seem important at the time. I couldn't have known how important those calls were. If I'd only taken them more seriously, maybe; but as they say: hindsight. It probably wouldn't have made a difference, or at least I try to believe that now.

It was almost noon before we arrived at the Command Post that Brad had set up at Custer's Real Estate office across the street from the gas station where Elsie Gilworth was last seen. The realtors had closed their business for the month of August and were getting ready for the fall season. They agreed to let the posse use the building.

The air was saturated with moisture, like swimming in a broccoli cream soup. At 115 degrees with a dry heat the temperature was unbearable, but with this humidity it was worse than hell.

Patty had parked her horse trailer under some shade trees along the side of the building. I saw Allen Cotton's red Silverado and four-horse trailer parked next to Jan's blue Eclipse. Some gossip's been going around about the two of them, but I don't believe a word of it. Allen always trailered horses for anyone who didn't have a rig.

We have a tight outfit. We don't always agree about politics and there have been some sticky situations in the marital realm, but if any posse member needs help, the rest of us are right there. Last year Kitty Beltran, one of our posse volunteers, had been severely injured in a traffic accident. She was in the hospital for more than a month. Kitty had always been the first to muster the members when anyone else needed a helping hand, so when she was laid up, everyone pitched in. Patty, who had some nursing training checked on Kitty every day until she was back on her feet. Brad arranged for volunteers to take her food after she got out of the hospital and Jan drove her to her doctor's appointments. All of us took turns taking care of Kitty's horses, but she had a parrot that didn't like strangers. After a few crunched fingers, I managed to make friends with the feathered fiend. Today I was afraid we might be dealing with a human fiend, and not one with whom I wanted to be a friend.

We pulled into the parking lot. "Sunshine, would you buy property from Custer's Real Estate?" Rick was in high spirits in spite of the heat.

"Well, the office is closed for the summer. Custer's last stand?" I quipped.

We walked into the realtor's office, now our CP. Rick placed his hand lightly on Brad's shoulder, "Hey, Brad. What can we do?"

Brad wiped his shirtsleeve at the sweat rolling down his face. "We've got another missing girl who fits the Whitewater Canyon victims' profile. Thirteen years old, brown hair, Caucasian. Parents say they had a fight about a boy she wanted to date. He was eighteen. They said no and she took off.

"They think she went to meet him. The girl's parents gave us his name and address. We talked to the young man. He said she called him and begged him to meet her at the gas station across the street from this office. According to him, she wasn't there when he drove in. The attendant at the station remembers a girl using the phone, but didn't see where she went after that. He confirmed that the boyfriend showed up later on looking for her."

Brad paused in his narration. "Sunny, Rick, thanks for coming. I need your help. I've been coordinating this search by myself and I'm running out of ideas, and to top it off, the refrigeration unit in this damn place isn't working." He turned to Rick, "We have four teams out already. Stay by the radio and keep track of the search teams. We've been running a schedule of two hours on and one off. This heat is killing us."

"Let me get Blackfoot out of the trailer and into some shade. I brought my own water barrel. You got a hook-up here?"

"Right over by the side of the building."

Brad's face was a little too ruddy. He looked like his blood pressure was going through the roof. "Sunny, take a look at this topo map." He thrust it into my hand. "Try to locate dirt or gravel roads adjacent to the highway."

Brad slammed his fist on the desk. "I don't want to find another victim of the Whitewater Canyon killer, but …"

"Okay, Brad." I unrolled the map onto the desk. Rick was looking over my shoulder at the topographical map that showed the natural and manmade features of the local area.

"Sunshine, you were about to tell me something and I cut you off. What was it?"

"What? Oh, I got another call from that phone freak."

"Did you get the number?"

"Uh huh. It's in our area. I know I've called that number before. It has to be someone I've talked with."

"Knowing you, Sunshine, you tried calling that number, right?"

"Yep, but there wasn't any answer. I looked up the prefix in the phonebook though. Whoever's making ·the calls lives in Palm Springs."

"Stupid pervert! Gets his kicks scaring helpless women and then hangs up."

Rick's comment hit me wrong. "He doesn't scare me, and I'm not helpless. Some jerk panting on the phone's not going to hurt me."

"Sorry, I didn't mean it that way."

"Never mind Rick. We have work to do." I tried to sluff it off, but Rick's comments offended me. I can take care of myself.

Two of the search teams came back to Command Post at noon. The horses were sweating heavily and the riders were exhausted; more from the ninety percent humidity than from the 115 degree heat.

Brad called the other two teams back in. "It's too dangerous for the horses and our people to work out in that extreme humidity and heat for more than a couple of hours at a time." He shook his head, "When the temperature drops, maybe we'll get back out there for another couple of hours before it gets dark."

The search turned up zilch. We all went home feeling sticky from the heat, and extremely tired. We'd expected to find Elsie Gilworth and hoped she would be alive, but after many long hours of intense searching, we didn't even find a trace. The posse had covered the area thoroughly; the only other likely possibility was abduction. If she'd gotten into a vehicle with someone, there was no way of knowing where she could be.

Chapter 43

Marietta Ranch

"Sunshine? Wake up! You're home." Rick was gently shaking me. Exhausted after the futile search for Elsie Gilworth, I'd fallen asleep on the drive back to the ranch.

"Sorry, I guess I wasn't very good company," I yawned.

"Don't give it a second thought. We're both tired, and to tell you the truth, I wasn't in the mood for conversation."

I found my ranch keys buried deep in my backpack and handed them to Rick. He got out of the truck and opened the gate. I was still half asleep and relieved to be home, familiar and comforting.

Rick walked me to the door, opened it, and gave me the keys. "It's been one hell of a day. Get some rest."

"Ummm," I mumbled. "You too."

I watched Rick drive slowly down the gravel driveway and closed the door of my adopted home on wheels.

A very annoyed Chowder kitty greeted me. She was determined to get my attention, rubbing against my legs and reminding me of the importance of a treat; preferably tuna, a proper penance for such neglect. I made sure that Chowder was munching on the best quality white flaked tuna before I called Laura to see how Shadow was doing.

"Laura, this is Sunny. Just got back. How's Shadow?"

"Sunny, I tried to call you. I didn't want to leave a message."

A sudden chill ran down my spine.

"Shadow's dead. I was so sure she was going to make it, but she just kept getting weaker. Her internal injuries were more serious than I thought. Every time I stopped the bleeding in one place, there was another that broke loose. I did my best to save her."

Tears were flowing down my cheeks, blurring my vision. "Shadow was so brave. She didn't deserve this."

"I'm so sorry, Sunny."

I put the phone down and just sat there, trying to make sense out of everything that had happened. We hadn't found Elsie Gilworth. Shadow was dead.

Chowder picked that moment to spring into my lap, almost as though she knew. "Oh Chowder ..." She rubbed against my hands as though she were stroking me, purring loudly. Suddenly she stopped. She leaped on the silent phone and knocked the receiver off the hook. I retrieved it from the floor. "You're right, Chowder. I'll get that sicky." My only lead was the weird phone calls. I had the number now. Maybe it was time to follow it through. "I'll find out who's been doing this, Chowder! Maybe I can't save Elsie Gilworth, but I can nail one asshole." I punched in the number that had shown up on Caller ID. It rang twice and a woman answered.

"Hello?"

I recognized the voice. "Madge?" My voice squeaked with shock.

"Yes, this is Madge."

I paused for a few seconds before I continued. "This is Sunny Morgan. I need to talk to you. Will you be home for a while?" There was hesitation obvious in her voice. "Sunny, it's late."

"It's very important, Madge."

"Well, can't you tell me over the phone?"

"No, I have to see you now."

Madge sighed, "I'll be here." Then I heard a click and a dial tone.

Chapter 44

Dry Springs Indian Reservation

"Grandfather Eagle, I desperately need your help."

"What is it Daniel?" The old eagle flapped his wings. "It has been a long time since you have called on me. I thought you had forgotten how to dream. You haven't gone beyond the second level in many moons."

"Grandfather, I have lost my way, my love, my family. What shall I do? My brother has chosen the dark way and he hates me because I ... he hates me because I exist."

"No, he is floundering about like a stupid fish trying to swim in air."

"But Grandfather, my Mary is dead. Antonio must be responsible for the witching that caused her death."

"Do not blame Antonio. It was a white man's demon who is to blame. Mary has long been in the afterworld, in Telmikish. She is one of the Nukatem, spirits of the first beings created by Mukat in the beginning. She was courted by your brother, Antonio, because he hoped to use her powers for his own purposes. She chose you and denied him. Like Tamaoit, Mukat's brother, he became jealous.

"She came to you in human form to turn your spirit for the good of your people. For all of your white man's learning, was it not she who guided you to teach the young people? Her spirit lives and guides you yet. She knows your ignorance of *The Path*. She came to you in a form you could accept."

"But Grandfather, I do not want to be a puul, a shaman."

"She knew this. It is your choice. But Grandson, a puul is not a white man's priest. You can use your powers for the good of the people. You can give them knowledge of the old ways; the language, the true path of your people.

"You have chosen to be a teacher of the old ways. You will search for the knowledge, the songs from long ago. It is your quest."

"But Grandfather, I am only a man. I ..."

"A puul does not wear black or deny his sexuality. You will know what to do. The Nukatem will guide you."

Daniel woke, drenched in perspiration. His head ached and tears flowed down his cheeks. "Oh Grandfather," he raised his hands above his head, "I am in pain. I suffer from my guilt and my loss."

He felt a cooling breeze as though from a fan of feathers. As he rose from his bed a single feather floated down into his hand. It was the feather of an eagle. "Thank you, Grandfather. I have heard you."

Daniel awoke from his dream again and again. With each awakening, the eagle feather was still in his hand.

Chapter 45

Twin Palms Sheriff Station

Mitch strode over to the desk and greeted the deputy on duty. "Hey Neely, what's up? Heard anything yet about the posse search for the Gilworth girl?"

"No, they're still looking." Sergeant Neely had a frown on his face. "Mitch, you asked me to check out the Wilson girl. As far as I can tell she never came through our department. I interviewed the parents. They insisted that she'd never been in trouble. There was one thing though. The mother said her daughter came home from school one day bubbling about two officers who came to her school to talk about being safe from strangers."

Mitch thought a moment; Jan Worthman's program. That could be the connection. "Thanks, Neely. Probably nothing to do with it, but you know how Jeff is."

"Yeah, he's stubborn about follow-up, that's for sure. Hope this helps with whatever you're working on. Jeff doesn't think any of us are involved with the Whitewater thing, does he?"

"Haven't got a clue. He's keeping his theories to himself. Just asked me to check it out." Mitch felt a shiver go down his neck. Daniel Martinez had said something when he was being questioned; it had prickled under his skin then. He tried to remember what it was.

Mitch called Jan Worthman's number. "Jan, this is Mitch Tolly."

"Hi Mitch."

"Do you remember doing a presentation at the school the Wilson girl attended?"

"Yeah, Deputy Branson and I went to Sagebrush Middle School together. He said he wanted to be a part of teaching the kids how to defend themselves."

"I'm surprised he took time to go with you."

"He must not have liked doing it. That was the only time he volunteered. After the abduction of the Wilson girl he said something about how my program didn't do any good and he wasn't going to waste his time. Really pissed me off."

"Don't let that jerk bring you down. What you're doing with the kids does make a difference. We're all behind your program."

"Thanks, Mitch. Listen, I've got to let you go. I've got a class at the Desert College tonight and I'm going to be late if I don't move it."

Mitch hung up the phone. He walked reluctantly back to Jeff's office to give him the report. The captain hadn't been too receptive lately.

"I think that just about clinches it." Jeff was tired beyond any tiredness he had ever felt before. "Now, Mitch, get over to the Beau Boutique and pick up Leonard Costa."

"Yes, Sir."

Chapter 46

Beau Boutique

Mitch parked his unmarked patrol car in a loading zone. Clouds cast fast moving shadows on the mountains; purples and reds and dark browns. The weatherman's forecast was for possible thunderstorms. Mitch cocked his head, breathed deeply, and thought there was no chance of rain today. He sauntered into Beau Boutique. The only customer had just picked up her packages and walked out the door. Lenny smiled and extended his hand. "Hi Officer Tolly. Can I help you find something? A gift perhaps?"

Mitch ignored Lenny's welcome. "Mr. Costa, this isn't a social call. We have some official business to discuss. I think you know what this is about." Mitch maintained a neutral expression. Lenny's face reddened. "Is there something more you need from me about Carrie's kidnapping?"

"Don't play games with me. What were you doing at the Stars Motel? You were seen coming out of a room where a murder was committed. Your car was identified. We can talk here or down at the station."

Lenny started to deny that he'd been at the motel, and then as if all the strength went out of his body, he crumpled into an antique chair. "All right, I was there. I went to talk to someone. When I got there, I found a body of a man. He was lying dead, his brains splattered all over. I thought it was the slimy snake who'd been threatening my wife. I called 911 and left. I didn't have anything to do with that man's death."

"It wasn't the man?"

"No. My wife received another threatening phone call after that."

"Why did you go to the motel in the first place?"

"My wife told me the man who threatened her was staying there."

"Let's stop the bullshit! Who is this guy who's threatening your wife, and what connection does he have with your daughter's kidnapping? You're going to tell me everything Costa, or I'll arrest you for impeding an investigation. I could take you in for suspicion of murder. Let's have the whole story."

Lenny took a deep breath and sighed. "Okay. This thing started a long time ago when my wife was in college. She was living with Greg Hanson. She told me that she got pregnant and he left her. Caroline and I had known each other for a while, and I was already in love with her, though I never thought she would return my feelings. She turned to me for help when she found out she was pregnant. I encouraged her to keep the baby and then, as she began to trust me, I asked her to marry me. I've never regretted the decision, not ever. Carrie has always known me as her father and I adore her."

"So you're a stand-up guy. What does all this ancient history have to do with you being at the scene of a homicide?"

"A few weeks ago my wife got a phone call from Greg Hanson. She hadn't heard from him for years, not since she found out she was pregnant. This jerk threatened to tell our daughter that I wasn't her father. He wanted money; a lot of money. He told her if we paid, he'd leave us alone. My wife went to the motel to talk to him. I didn't know anything about it then or I would have stopped her. My wife finally told me what happened. We discussed it and agreed we would not pay blackmail. He kept on harassing her. I was going to talk to him and convince him to leave us alone."

"Just talk?"

Lenny hesitated, "No, I took my gun with me. I was going to force him to leave my family alone one way or another. That's why I didn't stay. I was afraid I'd be arrested for killing him. I admit I was angry enough to do it. He deserved an assist to hell, but I didn't kill him. Check my gun. It hasn't been fired."

Mitch's expression hardened. "I'll do that. Where is it?"

"In our bedroom closet, top shelf."

"Not a very safe place to keep a gun when you have a child in the home."

Lenny exploded, "I'll take care of my family! You want information? Just get on with it!"

Mitch almost smiled. He'd get Costa to spill everything. "When you found out it wasn't this Greg Hanson guy who was killed, why didn't you report what you knew then? Why didn't you report the blackmail?"

"I thought we could handle it."

"Was it Greg Hanson who kidnapped your daughter?"

"I don't know."

"Would you recognize him?"

"No. It was a long time ago when I met him."

"Well, I presume if he is the father of her child, your wife would."

"Damn you! It's not like that."

Mitch smiled knowingly, "I need both of you to go over to the station and sign a statement. We need a description of the suspect. Your wife could help us put him away for life if she helps us identify him. Is there any reason you don't want her to do that?"

"No. You have to believe me. We were so grateful to have our daughter back safe. I guess I didn't think beyond that."

Mitch pointed his finger at Lenny. "I'd say you weren't thinking at all. You could have saved your wife and daughter a lot of trauma if you had come forward sooner. You're responsible for what happened to your daughter."

"You're out of your mind. None of this is my fault!"

"Close up the store. We'll go get your wife."

Lenny pushed himself out of the chair. He trudged out of the store and locked the door behind him. He appeared as fragile and aged as the antiques he sold.

Chapter 47

Marietta Ranch

An irritating, hot, desert wind rattled dried leaves in the rain gutters, and scratched bougainvillea thorns against the trailer's aluminum siding. The more I thought about those crank calls, the more furious I got. It was all beginning to make sense. I'd made an enemy when I told Jerry what I thought of him. Petty, vengeful jerk, he must have been the one breathing into the phone. My mind was shifting into warp drive. *So that's what Madge was worried about. She knew what he was doing. Well, I'm going to straighten this out right now,* I thought to myself. I started out the door then something made me turn around. I had to get my gun; this wasn't a scenario. This was the real thing and I'd better be prepared to protect myself.

The phone rang. "Hello."

"Sunny, this is Daniel."

"I can't talk right now. I have to go."

"Where are you going? You're in danger. Sunny wait for me at the ranch. I'm on my way."

"Daniel," I was exasperated. "I'm going to Madge Branson's. Meet me there if it's all that important." For one brief moment I hesitated. *What am I doing?* Then I gave Daniel the address, hung up the phone, and went out the door. Things might have turned out differently if I had stopped long enough to listen to Daniel.

The keys to the ranch van were in my purse. I locked the gun in the glove compartment and drove to the on-ramp for I-10. It's a thirty-five minute drive to the turn-off to Madge's house. I made it in twenty. I turned off the Tumbleweed exit and nearly missed the turn on to Coyote Drive. Madge's porch light was on. I parked the van at the curb and walked up the gravel path to the house.

Madge opened the door and stepped out on the porch before I had a chance to knock. Her mouth was scrunched into an attempted smile, but there was no smile in her eyes.

"Sunny, what on Earth?"

"That's what I'm hoping you can tell me. I've been getting weird phone calls and they came from your phone."

Madge backed up through the doorway. I followed her inside and closed the door behind me. She spoke in a hoarse voice, "Sunny, I've never called you, I wouldn't ..."

I didn't let her finish. "No, but Jerry did. You said he was upset and acting strange. You knew what he was doing to me, didn't you?"

Madge was cowering against the entryway wall. She raised her hands, protecting her face as though she thought I would strike her. I saw the silver pendant around her neck. It was identical to the one we found near Lindy Dibbs' body. "My God, Madge! Where did you get that necklace?"

"Bud gave it to me."

"Who's Bud?"

"Jerry, my brother Jerry. I always call him Bud. He gave it to me." She wrapped her long fingers around the amulet. "It was a present for my birthday."

"Madge!" I grabbed her hand. "What about the phone calls? You know about them, don't you?"

"Yes." Madge's voice was hoarse with emotion. "Something triggered this. Sunny, you did something that precipitated this mess. Bud's been all right for years. Why is it happening again?"

"What's happening again, Madge?" I tried to keep my voice steady.

She started sobbing, "It was so long ago. I was a young girl. I've tried to forget about poor Willy, but I can't."

"Willy?"

She hesitated. Her face contorted. I could see that the memory horrified her. "Willy was Bud's dog. I heard him whimpering under the porch. He saw me and came out dragging his hindquarters.

He had a wire tired around his back legs so tight that the circulation was cut off. He had deep cuts all over his poor body. He was slowly bleeding to death. Father took Willy out in the desert and shot him." Madge sadly shook her head. "Willy was a nuisance, a stupid mutt, but he didn't deserve to die like that. When father came back from the desert, he pistol-whipped Bud. He beat him until his back was black and blue. His face was so swollen that I thought father had broken his jaw."

Madge took a shaky breath. She gave me a look as though she was begging me to understand. "Later that night, I found Bud's bloody clothes when I was doing the laundry. He said the blood was from the beating, but I knew he was the one who'd tortured poor Willy."

Madge started pacing back and forth across the living room. She grimaced, "Bud was a nasty little boy, always peeking in my window when I was getting ready for bed. The bathroom door didn't have a lock. Bud would walk in on me when I was taking a shower. I thought he was just curious."

Madge scrutinized me carefully. "It was hard on all of us when mother left," she pleaded for understanding.

"One night, not long after Willy died, Bud crept into my room when I was asleep. He crawled under the covers and started touching me. At first it felt good, like in a dream, but when I woke up and realized what was happening, I told him to stop. He wouldn't. I scratched at his face and punched and kicked him until he left me alone. I was so ashamed. I thought it was my fault."

I put my arms around her and let her cry.

She shuddered involuntarily, "The next night he put a dead kitten under my pillow and stood in the doorway of my room, laughing while I screamed.

Bud said he'd kill me if I told. He never touched me again, but he came into my room at night after father had passed out from drinking. He described vividly and in horrible detail the animals he killed and tortured."

"God, Madge. You should have told someone."

"I was afraid to say anything. It wasn't until he set fire to a neighbor's storage shed that he got caught."

I tried to comfort her but Madge recoiled from my touch. "Madge?"

"Father said he could stay in juvenile hall for the rest of his life. He wouldn't let him come home. Bud went from one foster care home to another. Father started beating on me and I finally ran away. I was told that father died choking on his own vomit a few years later. I didn't cry. I came home for the funeral, got a job here and stayed."

"The past can cause great pain, but ..."

Madge looked at me with horror in her eyes. "It's starting again. Something isn't right with Bud. He doesn't come here often, but sometimes, I'm sure he's been here when I'm not home. I asked him about it but he just laughed. He told me I was paranoid. He said I should change the locks if it would make me feel better."

I stood there staring at her. The enormity of what I'd discovered left me speechless. I didn't think Madge had any idea about the implications of what she'd told me. She just looked at me, sobbing, her eyes red from crying. She wiped the mucous from her nose with the sleeve of her blue silk blouse and sank down on the couch with her head in her arms, emotionally exhausted.

I didn't have time to console her. I had to find out where Jerry lived. "Madge, I need to get to Jerry's place. Give me the address."

She looked at me like I was from outer space. "Madge! Now!"

"Just off the main road, 1235 Roadrunner Drive."

I regretted leaving Madge in such a bad situation, but I had to go. "Madge, Daniel Martinez works at the Marietta Ranch. He'll be here in a few minutes. Tell him that I've gone to your brother's."

I plunged out the door reeling down the walkway to the van. I forced my foot down on the accelerator and broke all the speed limits back to I-10.

Chapter 48

Twin Palms Sheriff Station

Smitty struggled with his anger. The Costas were not making it easy. "Okay, Mrs. Costa, we need your cooperation to set up a sting. The next time Greg Hanson calls you this is what you're going to do. Tell him you'll get the money. Let him pick a drop. We'll be listening on the line. He has to think you've finally given in and, in exchange for your peace of mind, you'll give him the cash."

"No, we won't do that!" Lenny shouted.

"You will do that! You'll go to jail for impeding an investigation if you don't!"

Caroline was in tears. "We'll do whatever you say. Lenny, please," she begged, "Carrie could have been killed. I don't want him to be loose out there."

Lenny looked at Caroline's stricken face.

"Oh, Lina. I ..." He turned to Smitty. "Do it."

"Good decision. The next time you might not be so lucky. Now go on home. We have the line tapped. He'll try again. He didn't go back to the shed where Carrie was kept prisoner. He may not even know she was rescued. Don't let on that Carrie is safe."

Caroline sighed wearily. "Please let Lenny go home. He didn't do anything. He was only trying to protect his family. He never killed anyone."

Smitty relaxed now that he had the plan in motion. "Yeah, I'll find someone to drive you home."

Chapter 49

Twin Palms Sheriff Station

The smell of autumn was in the air, reminiscent of the first day of school; still warm, but with just a hint of cooler weather coming. The leaves of a few trees not native to the desert were changing colors from green to gold.

Tiny Turner roared into the sheriff station parking lot, her Harley sparkling with chrome. "Okay, Otis, you can turn loose of my boobs. Not that it hasn't been fun."

A shaken Otis Grimes stuttered, "Tiny, can't you just once drive like a human being? I should have taken the deputy's offer to drive me in."

"God, Otis. You're such a wimp." Tiny was agitated, "All we have to do is go in and identify the guy who murdered your guest. You want to take a bus back, you're welcome."

Otis wiped the sweat off his face and carefully brought his leg over the cycle, "Tiny, you tried to freak me out!" Once his feet were on solid ground, Otis assumed a righteous stance. "Well, I guess you got your kicks, but remember, your rent could go up."

Tiny burst out in guffaws. "Bull! Otis, let's get this over with. Gimme my helmet. I don't want it ripped off while we're doing our duty as citizens." She marched up to the door, opened it, and with a wave of her hand scoffed, "You first, honey."

Tiny announced their mission to the desk officer and a deputy escorted them to a small room with a two-way mirror. Six men walked out. A voice ordered, "Number one, step forward. Turn to the right. Turn to the left."

Otis whispered, "No, that's not him."

Tiny laughed loudly, "God, Otis. He can't hear you."

The voice called out, "Number two, step forward. Turn right. Turn left."

Otis frowned at Tiny and growled loudly, "Not him!"

The voice ordered, "Number three, step forward."

Tiny squealed, "That's him! That's the dude who gave me the booze. He's the one all right. I'd know that face anywhere. What a waste."

Otis confirmed that number three was the man who rented room twenty six.

"Deputy, can we get out of here now?" She grabbed Otis by the arm. "Com'on honey. Let's go have some fun. I'll pay the tab."

Otis simpered, "Tiny, just take it a little easy, will yuh?"

"Sure, honey. Don't sweat it. I may wear the pants, but I let you wear the helmet, don't I?"

Chapter 50

Twin Palms Sheriff Station

Greg Hanson and five other prisoners were in the lineup. Greg was number three. Carrie fidgeted while Caroline and Lenny sat behind the two way mirror looking at the men as the deputy called each one to come forward. When number three was called, Carrie heard her mother gasp, grabbed her arm, and shook it fiercely. "Mom, that's him, isn't it?"

"That's Greg Hanson!" Caroline blurted out. "He called me and demanded money!" Caroline's eyes flashed angrily. She hugged Carrie. "You recognized him?"

Carrie began to cry and then sobbed into her mother's breast. She moaned, "He's the one who broke into Sunny's trailer. Mom he's the one who hurt Sunny."

Caroline bristled with anger. "Officer, the kidnapper is number three. He's the bastard who kidnapped and tormented my daughter." She paused briefly, "I know him. He's the man who tried to extort money from me."

The officer took down the information from a not-too-rational Caroline and then escorted the Costas out of the room. I'll have a statement for you to sign in a few minutes, Mrs. Costa. You and your daughter may have to testify, but your identification should be enough to put that scum away for life."

Lenny's face contorted with rage. "I'd like just five minutes with that slimeball! After what he's done to my family, he shouldn't have a life! I never believed in the death penalty before, but that puking predator changed my mind. I wish I'd found him first!"

Caroline put her arms around Carrie and Lenny and held them close. "It's over Lenny. Just be glad it's over now. I love you both so much. We'll be okay now."

Carrie wrested away from her mother. "Mom, why did you let that man kidnap me? Sunny said he used to be your friend. I don't understand."

Caroline embraced her daughter. "Carrie, I would have given my life if this hadn't happened. I don't understand it myself. There's something twisted inside Greg. He has too much hate boiling inside him and it made him do terrible things. I love you." Caroline pleaded, "Please believe me, your dad and I will always love you."

A police officer came in with a statement for the Costas to sign. "I'm Sergeant Joseph Brody from the Palm Springs Police Department. Read this over and sign here." He pointed to a place on the paper marked with an 'X'. "That's it for now, but we may need to interview you again." He smiled at Carrie who still had tears streaming down her cheeks. "Thank you for your help, young lady."

Carrie's sobs suddenly ceased. With a searching expression, she demanded, "Can girls be police officers?" Carrie scrutinized the officer's face for an answer.

For a moment the officer was taken aback by Carrie's newly composed attitude. He glanced at Caroline and Lenny, observed Lenny's nod and replied in a very serious voice, "Sure they can. Stay in school. Get good grades and when you graduate, you could go to the academy or take law enforcement classes in college."

"I want to ride horses and be in the sheriff's posse when I grow up."

"Sure, little lady, you can do anything if you put your mind to it. Our police chief is a woman and she's very good at her job!"

"I just wanted to be sure. My teacher said women shouldn't have jobs where they carry guns. He says I should be an accountant because I'm good with numbers. I don't want to be an accountant." Carrie paused, "Officer Brody, I've met you before, haven't I?"

Sergeant Brody grinned, "Yep. I was first on the scene after you and Ms. Morgan escaped from the kidnapper."

Carrie nodded thoughtfully, "I remember you. Officer Brody, will you write a recommendation for me when I go to the academy?"

Caroline interrupted, "My daughter is only eleven years old going on twenty one. She has no idea what she wants to do when she grows up."

"Mom!"

"Carrie, be reasonable. You can't possibly want to be in law enforcement."

"I know what I want to do! Mom, I know." Carrie ardently begged the officer, "Please Officer Brody, will you?"

Joseph Brody was confronted with a choice. Would he back up the parent, or would he follow his heart? Something about this girl struck a special note with him. He saw the antagonism on Carline's face and then glanced at the girl. *I may be sorry for this,* he thought. "You bet, Miss Costa. In a heartbeat!"

Caroline drew in a deep breath and swallowed her disparaging words before they were spoken. "Thank you Officer Brody, perhaps someday …"

Chapter 51

Twin Palms Sheriff Station

It was just about time for the afternoon shift to leave. Smitty charged into Jeff Newhouser's office. Jeff was on the phone. "Yes, I appreciate your call. We will keep you informed." Jeff scowled, "Yes, sir. Yes, I know who you are. Yes. Well, do what you need to do. I'm the Captain here." Jeff kept his cool. "Your son's in custody because we have evidence he committed a crime." Jeff slammed the phone down and snapped, "What now?"

"Damn it, Jeff. I wouldn't bust in here if it weren't important. We've got a connection between the Stars Motel murder and the Costa kidnapping. Tiny Turner and Otis Grimes fingered Greg Harwin as the suspect in the motel murder. The thing is, the Costas know the suspect as Greg Hanson. They say he's the guy who kidnapped their daughter. Tobias Black knows him as Handy Miller. This dude is the son of Judge Hanson. God! You can expect a slew of attorneys here any minute." Smitty shook his head. "If the media gets hold of this story, nobody's going home anytime soon."

Jeff pointed to the phone. "I already got my first blast form the judge. Damn it, Smitty." He smiled menacingly. "I hope the case against his son is ironclad."

Smitty smiled, "Jeff, the guy is a goner, son of a ..." he paused meaningfully, "son of a judge or not."

"Good. It gives me great pleasure to shake that tree. Smitty, I need the full report on my desk, ASAP!"

"You got it!" Smitty quietly walked out of the office, a victorious grin on his face. He couldn't resist, "By God, sometimes the bad guys do get caught by their short hairs."

Jeff heard him and thought *Yep, but it isn't going to be easy.*

Deputy Carl Diaz bumped into Smitty and stalked into Jeff's office, an impatient look on his face.

"You wanted to see me?"

"Just a minute."

"I'm in a hurry Captain. I'm off duty as of ten minutes ago." Diaz's mouth contorted into an insolent sneer. "Whaddya want? Can't it wait?"

The Captain heaved an exasperated sigh. "No, dammit, it can't. Were you working security at the last Indian Fiesta?"

"Nothing wrong with that, is there?"

"Look Carl, I don't approve of moonlighting, but I can't stop you. Were you?"

"Yeah. Me and Jerry Branson. We both needed the money."

"Did either of you buy a pendant like this from one of the booths?" Jeff casually put a photograph of a pendant with Indian designs on the desk.

"We didn't buy them. The guy gave them to us. Said it was for luck, bad luck most likely. I didn't want it. It was a toad pendant just like that one; creepy. I gave mine to Jerry. He said his sister would like it. What's the big deal?"

"Carl, I'll bet you kept the money."

"What money?"

"Don't bother denying it. If you paid any attention to what has been going on around here, you'd know that piece of jewelry was critical to an ongoing investigation." Newhouser threw a pendant down on his desk. "This was found near one of the Whitewater killer's victims. I put out a memo to everyone about it."

"Well, I didn't get no memo. And for the record, there wasn't no money."

"I'm not going to argue with you. Write up a statement about everything you remember that happened at that fiesta. Have it on my desk before you leave today."

"Captain," Carl Diaz snarled, "I've had it with this department. All I get is hassles from you. First bugging me about a couple of shotguns and then complaining about my time off. Now all this shit about some stupid necklace. I want a transfer."

"Put your request in writing, Diaz. I'm sure it can be arranged, that is if you can make it past the Internal Affairs investigation. And

Diaz, I want an explanation about the money that came with the pendant."

Diaz's face registered shock when he heard Jeff's demand. "I quit." He stomped out of the office.

Mukat's Heart: A Sunny Morgan Mystery

Chapter 52

Madge Branson's Residence

Madge Branson's hair, usually so tightly controlled, was flying wildly about her head. Her face was contorted, swollen and red by an unrestrained flood of tears. In frenzy, she tried to swallow a handful of pills. Daniel knocked them from her hands. Screaming and clawing at Daniel's face, Madge struggled ferociously as Daniel held her until she finally surrendered and collapsed in a heap on the couch.

Daniel listened to Madge's raving on and on about wanting to die. At last, he gently cradled her face with his fingers and quieted her. He convinced the still weeping woman to tell him where I had gone, and then he grabbed the phone and called the Sheriff Station.

Jerry answered the phone, "Deputy Branson."

Daniel spoke forcefully, "Find Sergeant Tower right away. I must talk to him."

Jerry recognized Daniel's voice and got an odd look on his face. "May I ask who is calling?"

"Is he there or not?" Daniel was impatient, not willing to give his name.

"Yes, I'll connect you."

"Sergeant Tower. May I help you?"

"Rick, you have to trust me on this one. I am at Jerry's sister's house right now. She's having some kind of mental breakdown. She's rambling on about some phone calls. She's blaming Sunny for all kinds of horrible things. I don't think you better let Jerry know about this right now. I have a bad feeling that Madge is the caller that's been harassing Sunny. Can you get over here? I think you should talk to Madge. I have to get going. Sunny's on her way to …"

"I have a couple of things I have to do here first then I'm on my way." Rick didn't wait for Daniel to finish talking before he hung up the phone. He didn't hear the click on the other end after Daniel hung up the phone.

Rick grabbed a stack of papers and rushed through them. He had to finish the paperwork on two arrests and then he'd go over to Madge Branson's house; although for the life of him he didn't understand what the hurry was. Sunny must have found out who had been making the kinky calls. Daniel and Sunny shouldn't have to deal with Jerry's sister. He'd better let Jerry know that his sister was freaking out. When Rick got to the front office, he saw Deputy Branson hastily leaving his desk.

About five minutes later, Jeff Newhouser walked up to Rick. He had a worried look on his face. "Rick, have you seen Jerry around?"

"He was at his desk a minute ago, Jeff. What's up?"

"Rick, I got an ID on the deputies who were at the Indian Fiesta. It was Jerry Branson and Carl Diaz. They were doing security there. I can understand why Diaz didn't want to talk, but damn it all, I want to know why Jerry didn't come forward with the information himself. I put out a memo. Mitch and Smitty said they talked to every deputy here. They came up with nothing. They must have talked to Jerry. Find him! I want Branson in my office pronto."

"You got it Jeff. I'll find him." Rick put aside the reports and went looking for Jerry. He glanced outside and noticed that Jerry's truck was gone from the parking lot. That's strange, he thought. First, Daniel did not want Jerry to know about his sister, and now the Captain wanted to talk to him. Jerry's supposed to be on duty tonight. Why would he leave so early?

"Jeff, it looks like Jerry took off. His truck isn't in the lot. What's going on here?"

"I don't know Rick, but I'm beginning to think that Jerry's involved somehow with the Whitewater Canyon case. It's a possibility that he knows the killer."

"Jeff, Daniel just called me. He thinks Madge Branson has been making harassing calls to Sunny Morgan. This is a connection that could endanger Sunny. I need to know! There may be more to this than the phone calls."

"I'm not sure, maybe it's just a breakdown in communication. Jerry never has been very forthcoming, but ..."

Jeff Newhowser was still talking when Rick rocketed out of the straight backed chair.

"Jeff, I'm taking a patrol car to Madge Branson's place. Get me some back up."

The underarms of Rick's shirt were wet. *Damn it! Sunny's gotten herself into a dangerous situation.* Rick charged out of the office. *How could I have missed it? Stupid! Damn it all to hell!*

Chapter 53

My hands gripped the steering wheel so tightly my fingers were white. *God, I hope I'm not too late. There's no time to call for back up and besides, there's a chance it would alert Jerry if I call into the station. Daniel will follow me. That should be enough. I have to stop Jerry.*

There was a wind advisory sign posted on I-10. The van was buffeted into the slower traffic lane, almost hitting a semi grinding up the steep grade. My headlights reflected off the sand that was blowing across the freeway and almost blinded me. I nearly missed the Yucca Valley turn off. I swerved, tires squealing, just in time to make the off-ramp for Highway 62. Traffic was light this late at night, but the few cars on the road all had their bright lights on making visibility worse.

Can't see! Have to slow down!

A fierce gust of wind forced me to fight the steering wheel. What I wouldn't give to be driving the old Toyota. This van drives just like a kite in the wind.

The long stretches of Highway 62 are treacherous, even in daylight. I had driven this road at night before. Curves appeared unexpectedly as I drove up the steep grade to the high desert town of Yucca Valley. It started to rain; light spattering at first and then the cloudburst beat down against the windshield, too much for the wipers to clear away.

"Damn, not rain! It's like the gods themselves are against me. I can't see the road." I had started talking to myself out loud. "Slow down, wait it out, too dangerous," I worried but continued to accelerate. Just as quickly as it began, the rain stopped. Torrents of water poured down the sides of the rocky hills onto the road. I saw the red and blue flashing lights just in time to avoid the two wrecked cars ahead; one turned over in the road and the other off the side.

Shit! I took a deep breath. *That could have been me.* I took my foot off the accelerator.

The highway patrol was already on the scene. One officer used his flashlight to wave me on around the accident, but not before giving me a warning. "Miss, you need to be more careful. I should give you a ticket."

"Sorry officer." I gave him a chagrined smile.

I drove more carefully, but still faster than the speed limit. The road was slick from the recent rain mixed with oil that accumulates during a long drought. I almost went over the edge on the last tight curve, but managed to slide back onto the road. The town of Yucca Valley was in sight, but there were so many side roads and the sign were impossible to see. *Roadrunner Drive, where are you?*

I drove slowly through the town and turned around. Rain water was rushing down the sides of the road, reflecting the reds and blues of neon lights flashing from closed business. I turned around again, frustrated. The street signs were too small to read easily from the dark street. I went all the way through the town again and turned back, once more trying to find a small side street that probably didn't even have a sign.

What was that song? Daniel had taught me a song of finding. He sang it to me in the Cahuilla language and then translated it into English. I tried to remember the Cahuilla, but couldn't. A chanting began in my mind.

Show me what is to be found. I am here. I am looking. Show me what is to be found.

With my hand I wiped away a think mist that had formed on the inside of the windshield. I turned on the wipers and finally cleared the glass. There it was. Lights from a gas station illuminated the sign, 'Roadrunner Drive.' The dirt and gravel road was steep, winding up the side of a hill. The rain had made deep furrows down the middle and I stayed to one side hoping to avoid the potholes and not slide in the mud. I fought the steering wheel, keeping the van in low gear, not daring to stop.

1215 on that mailbox. Jerry's place had to be close. I passed several cabins that looked vacant, and then drove through a cleared area with some old water tanks.

Rain began to pour again. A flash of lightning lit up the empty driveway for a brief moment. I could barely see the black mailbox on the side of a narrow gravel road, but the flaking silver decals were reflected by my headlights.

There it is. 1235!

The cabin, almost hidden by Palo Verde trees, was set back from the road with a narrow driveway leading to a covered carport. No lights or vehicles were in sight. *Phew.* I exhaled with relief. *Jerry's not here.*

I began to wonder if I'd jumped to conclusions. *Sure Jerry's a jerk, but a serial killer?* Madge is as strange as Jerry. Maybe she concocted that story to get back at him. Could she have been the one who made those calls? Her voice was deep enough to be mistaken for a man. This could be her version of a snipe hunt. "No!" I said aloud. "I saw the amulet around Madge's neck. It's gotta be him! But could Madge …"

I parked the van, unlocked the glove compartment, took out the Glock, and tucked it into the back of my jeans. I put on my rain jacket to hide the gun. Then I checked the flashlight. The batteries were still good. My muscles ached. I climbed wearily out of the van.

The rain let up again, at least for the moment, but the rain-soaked mud-sloshed into my high top sneakers. Still, they gave me enough traction so I didn't slip as I squished my way cautiously up to the cabin.

Not a sign of anyone. The door was locked. I worked my way around the cabin, checking the windows. At the back, one window was slightly open; maybe an inch, but an inch was all I needed. I pulled the screen out, pushed the window up far enough to crawl inside, and turned on the small flashlight to investigate. The light wasn't enough to illuminate the entire area. I saw a pleasant room with a brown leather couch in front of a small fireplace. A glass-covered bookcase filled with Indian artifacts covered one wall from floor to ceiling. It was slightly askew. I brought the light closer and found an opening in the wall behind.

"That's odd." I pulled on the bookcase. It moved easily on oiled hinges, revealing a hidden room. The first things my light caught were the oil paintings. One was of a partially nude Indian woman. Three more showed naked children in grotesque poses. Unbelieving, I moved closer and aimed the flashlight at one of the paintings. At the lower right side of the canvas was the flamboyant signature of Buddy Branson. The smell of paint thinner permeated the air. I walked quietly around the small room. I found an easel covered with a white cotton cloth. I carefully lifted the cloth.

The oil painting was unfinished, but there was no doubt that a young girl had been the model. Her mouth was open, screaming. I shivered uncontrollably. He was skillful, a gifted artist, but his subject matter turned my stomach. I recognized Elsie Gilworth. There were other canvasses leaning against the wall: The Wilson girl and Lindy Dibbs with her party hat. There was another one. I shuddered.

My God, it's Mary Martinez.

The resemblance was extraordinary. I was looking at an artist's gallery of the dead.

My stomach got the best of me and I vomited all over the bold designs of a large Navajo rug, but some detached part of my mind continued thinking. *Odd, how can Jerry afford a carpet like this?* It would be more his style to own an orange and yellow shag rug.

I froze at the soft sounds of footsteps behind me.

"Ah, Sunny, you came to have your portrait painted." Jerry's voice was thick, unctuous with an ugly sensuousness.

I whirled around and saw a pistol pointed at my chest.

"You don't seem to be feeling well. Maybe you should sit down over there." He waved his gun toward a straight back chair. He turned on a small lamp, opened the drawer of an antique roll top desk. A set of handcuffs glinted in the light. "My models have to sit very still, Sunny." Jerry pushed the barrel of the gun against my breast. "Sit down!"

I sat.

"As you can see, I haven't quite finished my latest work." I could hear his heavy breathing as he nuzzled his face in my hair, gently bringing my arms behind the chair and handcuffing my wrists to the back of the chair.

"Jerry, I …"

"I've never had an audience before. I hope you enjoy the experience of watching a great artist at work." He stroked my face and left the room. I was repulsed by his touch, but I couldn't believe my luck. Jerry was so distracted and physically aroused that he didn't notice the Glock stuck in the waistband of my jeans. I breathed a silent sigh of relief. My jacket must have hidden it from view.

I tried to reach the gun through the opening in the back of the chair. My mind was entirely focused on survival. I had to get the gun.

Just a little more, if I could just slide the cuff chain a little more.

Jerry came back carrying Elsie. She was drugged, almost unconscious. He placed the girl on a small sofa in front of the easel and meticulously arranged her naked body. Caressing her long brown hair, he spread it over a small white velvet cushion. "There," he murmured, "you will be beautiful forever. My genius will make you immortal." He turned to me, the pupils in his eyes dark and large. "You see Sunny, I have the power now. It was too late for Madge. I didn't know how to save her then."

"Jerry, when did you do the painting of Mary?" I wasn't sure how he would respond. If I ever got out of this alive, I had to know if Jerry had murdered her and why.

"Name's Buddy." Jerry had a puzzled expression on his face. "Jerry's kind'a fuzzy, lost in a fog. Stupid Jerk!" His face hardened.

The self-satisfied announcement of his name was bizarre. I felt a prickling of terror at the back of my neck.

It was Buddy who continued, "Things happened to me that I didn't understand. I lost whole days of my life. One night I woke up. Years had gone my. I didn't know where I was at first. I was wearing a deputy sheriff's uniform and I was in a small palm frond hut with an Indian shaman. He touched my forehead and said that he'd been waiting for me."

Jerry's eyes were without expression; it was as though he were narrating a story about somebody else. "After a few sessions with the shaman I learned to control my time and learned about the last twenty years that were stolen from me.

"The shaman revealed to me that I had a special talent that was struggling to emerge. I hadn't realized until then that everything had been predestined. He introduced me to Mary Canyon and asked me if I would paint her portrait. He promised that he would protect me, but only if the portrait I painted of her was perfect.

"I spent days planning her pose, setting up the background, arranging each fold of her clothes. She smile and laughed with me. I was elated, sure that at last I would be recognized as a great artist and she would be the one to inspire me with her beauty. But after the portrait was finished she said it was going to be her wedding present for her fiancé. She couldn't give that portrait away. It was the price I had to pay for my freedom.

"You understand, don't you Sunny? Then she said she was marrying Daniel Martinez. Liar!" Jerry's face was brilliant red. "I didn't believe it, so that night I waited outside her house. Daniel drove up. Mary came out to greet him and they went into her house. I watched them; Mary and that pervert, Daniel, in bed. Screwing. Obscenity after obscenity."

Jerry put his gun down and began painting on the unfinished canvas. "I had to kill her. All smiles and underneath was a whore. I told Antonio. He said he had a vision. I must forget about the portrait and I must return all the artifacts that I purchased from my contact or Buddy Branson would be lost in oblivion. He'd pay me well for them. He did, too, but it didn't stop me. Not even Antonio could do that. I kept the portrait."

Oh shit! My thoughts were racing. Daniel warned me, but even he couldn't have known that his brother had created a madman with his dark magic. I'd thought I could convince Jerry with reason, but now I genuinely began to fear for my life.

Jerry's voice exploded with maddened power. He stared at me. "My art will make me a God. With my brush and canvas I can save all the children and never be lost in the darkness again."

I found that I could move my hands. If only the chain on the cuff was long enough, maybe I could reach my gun. I carefully tried to maneuver the chain as quietly as I could. My heart was pounding so loudly I was sure Jerry would hear. I have to get out of here! An ironic thought calmed me down. I grimaced, I really didn't want my portrait painted; I didn't even like to be photographed. The chain slid a little more. My confidence returned.

Jerry continued to talk with maniacal religious fervor, "Antonio rubbed his hands together and then opened them. There was a small black stone in his left hand. He gave it to me and told me to swallow it. He held both his arms above my head and whispered to me that all I had to do was lay with Mary once, take her, and then ..." Jerry's tirade stopped and he stared at something beyond the canvas. "Then Antonio drew a picture of a toad in the sand and told me to carve its likeness on Mary's door. He promised she would do whatever I wished. He lied.

"When I asked her to have sex with me, she laughed at me. I tried to explain to her that she had a duty, but she screamed and scratched my face. She wasn't worthy of my seed! I took her portrait away with me. I had to save her as I will save you when I finish this." Jerry stopped talking and focused on his subject.

I shuddered violently. The man was psychotic; his thinking totally bizarre. What on earth had Daniel's brother been trying to do? Did he set all these vicious killing sin motion? Did he know that Jerry, sick in the mind as he was, would kill Mary? The terrible things that Jerry had done to his victims rushed through my mind. How could he possibly believe he was saving them when he raped, tortured, and murdered them?

Jerry turned his attention away from me and began to concentrate totally on his painting. Elise was beginning to move a little and Jerry went over to her to reposition an arm. I slid the chain of the handcuffs to one side and slowly got my fingers around the butt of the gun. I slipped it out. Jerry was moving toward the easel when he saw the gun in my hand. He lunged toward me. I angled the gun and got off a shot. It hit him low, in the leg. He kept coming, reaching out to grab me. I shot again, a little higher this time. The bullet hit him in the chest. I fired once more, this time into his groin. He crumpled onto the floor.

"Sunny, you shouldn't have done that," he gasped. "I could have saved you, too." Blood trickled from his mouth, and then he was still, his eyes still open, staring sightlessly.

I dropped the Glock. I'd taken a life. Jerry was a detestable, vicious man, obviously deranged, but he was still a human being. I didn't even try to get out of the chair. I sat there in shock staring at Jerry's dead body. That was how Daniel found me; sitting and staring.

Chapter 54

Rick knocked on the door of Madge Branson's house. There was no answer, and Daniel's truck was nowhere around. The door was open. "Madge? Sunshine? Daniel?" His hand on his weapon, he eased through the door. "Anyone here?" He saw a figure laying half on the couch and half on the floor. He went quickly to Madge. She had a faint pulse. She was unconscious. Her breathing was very slow and shallow. Then Rick saw the empty pill bottle. "Seconal! Damn!" He grabbed the phone. "This is Deputy Tower. I have a female in respiratory distress. She appears to have ingested an unknown number of Seconal capsules." He gave the address and said, "Get an ambulance here pronto. I don't know when she took the pills or how many."

The paramedics were putting Madge on the stretcher when Rick saw the pendant. His worst fears were confirmed.

He picked up the phone and placed a call, this time to headquarters.

Deputy Smith answered.

"Smitty, Madge Branson tried to commit suicide. The ambulance has taken her to Desert Dunes Hospital. She was wearing a pendant like the one we found near the Dibbs' body. Give me Jerry Branson's home address."

Chapter 55

Marietta Ranch

I was home again, what was left of me. Case closed. There would still be an investigation of Jerry Branson's death, but it was only perfunctory; just a matter of routine and procedure. We never heard anything more about the disc I found near Lucy Martinez's remains. Greg Hanson was found guilty of murder and kidnapping. His father, the Judge, was found dead, apparently from a heart attack. The tribes completed negotiations with the governor on a gaming compact. Nobody except Daniel believed anything I said about Antonio Martinez's role in Mary Canyon's death.

I was sitting at the kitchen table in the dawn light with Chowder on my lap when there was a knock at the door. I picked Chowder up in my arms and opened the door to find Rick standing there, a look of concern on his face.

"Sunshine, are you up to a little company?"

"Rick, I don't need any company, but I sure do need to talk to you."

"That's why I'm here. You've been through a lot," He stood uncertainly outside the doorway. "I thought maybe I could help you work through some of what happened. I've been there."

"Come on in." I felt a genuine sense of relief.

Rick hugged me gently. "Hey, you have any coffee hot?"

"I'll make a fresh pot. I'm glad you're here. I can't stop thinking about murder and death."

Chowder was still purring when I put her down on the cushion of my favorite chair. I know from the orange hairs that she takes possession of it during the day if I'm not home.

I ground some Kenya coffee beans and started the coffee maker. "Rick, how was it possible for Jerry to have become a law enforcement officer? I just don't understand. With all the things he did, how did it happen?"

"Jerry was a minor when he was first arrested. He was never convicted of any crime as an adult and his juvenile records were sealed. The way the department shrink explained it to me was that Jerry must have so totally closed off that part of his life that he himself didn't even remember what he'd done. His theory is that Jerry suffered from Multiple Personality Disorder."

Sunny shook her head in disbelief, "But Rick, I know the department demands a lot of testing to weed out the weirdoes."

"None of the psychological testing done when Jerry was an adult showed any problems. Recently, there had been so many stresses on him that at some point he went over the edge; lost control. The new persona he'd constructed crumbled."

"But ..." Sunny shuddered, "but what about Antonio Martinez? Remember what I told you about his part in Mary's murder?"

"No proof, Sunshine. Just more evidence that Jerry Branson was mentally ill."

"Daniel believes it."

"Psychic garbage!" Rick laughed. "Don't let yourself get sucked in. Jerry Branson was a sicko, pure and simple."

"I don't know how I feel about him, Rick. He was such a monster. Part of me is glad I killed him, but ..."

"Sunshine, you didn't have a choice. You did the right thing; you and Elsie came out of that house alive. You can have compassion for the terrible childhood that he and his sister endured. Don't take this wrong, but you really should have called for backup before you took off. You could have been another of his victims. Not even an experienced officer ought to approach a homicide suspect without calling for backup."

"Don't start on that again. I didn't know for sure that he was the killer and I did tell Daniel where I was going."

"No, you told Madge to tell Daniel where you were going. It isn't the same thing. It was just luck that he found you."

"Rick, who's side are you on anyway? You're just giving me more to blame myself for. I don't need this." I pushed Rick's hand away from my shoulder.

"Sunshine, you have to look at the events realistically. You didn't do anything wrong. There are some things I wish you'd done to ensure your safety, but there weren't any guarantees. You did fine. I'm not criticizing you. You already had the situation under control before Daniel got there. I think what I'm trying to tell you, is you're not alone here. Give me a chance to help. I care a lot about you, lady."

I held back the tears that threatened to fall. "Rick, stop I can't take any more. You'd better go."

"Okay but there's one more thing that you ought to know. Madge *was* the one making those calls. Jerry told her about the girls and what he did to them. He was terrorizing her just like he did when they were children. That's why she tried to kill herself. He threatened to kill her if she told. She kept trying to get the courage to tell you who was torturing and murdering those girls. Unfortunately, she wasn't able to overcome her fear."

"Rick, please! I can't stand to hear any more of this. I know you're trying to help, but I just can't deal with this right now."

"I'll go. When you're ready to talk, call me. Oh, by the way, my wife just filed for a divorce." Rick left without looking back at Sunny.

Oh, Rick, I wanted to shout, *I'm sorry.* I wanted to go after him and tell him to hold me and help make it all go away. Instead, I just stood there watching him walk out the door and maybe out of my life.

Mukat's Heart: A Sunny Morgan Mystery

Chapter 56

October 1999
Marietta Ranch

October in the desert promises an end to searing humid days. Skies are so blue and clear that it is impossible to stay inside, and nights are cool enough to require a down comforter. Despite the fall splendor descending on the desert, I was as grumpy as a bear coming out of hibernation. The depression that overwhelmed me after I killed Jerry was still hovering like a dark cloud.

I hadn't gone on a call-out with the posse since everything came down, and Max was getting fat from inactivity. Chowder followed me everywhere, her tail twitching anxiously. She worried when I went into the bathroom, scratching at the door until I came out. When I got in the old Toyota, she jumped onto my lap. I finally had to lock her in the trailer before I could leave the ranch. At night, she lay across me, making it impossible to even turn over. I think she was grieving for Shadow as much as I was. She did have some mercy on me in the mornings. Uncharacteristically considerate, she let me sleep in. I was swimming in a heavy black emotional soup. If I could have, I would have slept for the rest of my life. Loaded with Zanax, I didn't dream; or at least I didn't remember my dreams. I dragged through the days, longing for my work on the ranch to be over so I could sleep.

The phone rang and rang. I'd shut off my answering machine. This time I picked up the phone just to make it stop ringing. "Hello."

"Sunny! This is Laura. Thank goodness I got through. I've been trying to call you for days." Laura paused. "I know how much you must miss Shadow. I really tried my best to save her."

"I know you did, but I just can't talk about it right now."

"Sunny, I have a big favor to ask. A couple of volunteer firemen brought in a German Shepherd puppy rescued from a fire up in the Pinyon area. She had an infected paw. I think she got caught in a coyote trap. She's healing well. Her fur is badly singed, but it will grow back. I can't find anyone to take her. If she isn't adopted in the next two days she'll be destroyed."

"I don't know if I can help you Laura. I can't even take care of myself."

"I know you're having a rough time, Sunny, but this dog needs someone desperately. She's a little frightened right now, but she's a fine animal, and she's young enough to overcome the trauma she's been through. I just can't let her be put down, not if there's a chance she could have a good home."

"I'll come over and take a look, that's all I'll promise."

"You won't be sorry. This puppy is really special. She's been through a lot, but her great heart shines through. I'd take her home myself if I could."

"Tomorrow Laura. I'll drive over there tomorrow. Okay?"

Laura paused briefly, "Sunny ... If you'll let me, I'll bring her over to the ranch myself. You don't even have to drive out here."

I didn't want Laura to come, but I didn't have the energy to resist her determination. "Okay. Tomorrow."

In my dreams that night, Shadow came to me whining, wagging her stumpy tail, and barked twice. A small German Shepherd puppy wiggled up to her. Shadow licked the puppy and turned to me with luminescent eyes, pleading. "All right Shadow, I'll do it. For you, I'll do it."

I woke up still feeling Shadow's soft tongue licking my hand.

Chapter 57

October 15, 1999
Marietta Ranch

Leon came back to work, a little quieter; even more inclined to solitude than before, but back to work. We tried to talk a couple of times, but somehow the words just didn't come, and we worked together without discussing the kidnapping. Neither of us could get beyond the fact that Leon hadn't warned me about Greg Hanson. We both knew Carrie and I could have died because he hadn't told me. I didn't want to lose his friendship. How could he have known what would happen?

When I first started work at the Marietta, Leon was determined to rescue me; but now, when I needed his friendship the most, he acted like I didn't even exist.

I'd been to the Department shrink, angry and depressed. Yes, Elsie Gilworth was alive, but I'd killed a human being. My sessions with the counselor helped, the anti-depressants helped, but it was my time with Daniel that gave me permission to forgive myself.

I spent most of my days off at the Reservation Community Center. One morning, he called me and insisted that I come to his home on the reservation. "Daniel, I thought you had to go to Sacramento."

"The meeting was canceled at the last minute. Meet me at my place in an hour."

I drove slowly past the Community Center which was buzzing with activity. The Center's committee members and a flurry of excited children were erecting a sign that welcomed all to attend the Cahuilla Children's Art Festival.

Daniel was waiting for me outside his adobe house. "Sunny, I'm glad you could make it!"

"Are we going to the art show?"

"Tomorrow, Sunny. The kids are just setting up. I have something else in mind."

Daniel didn't seem his usual self. More forceful somehow, but I was intrigued. "And what might that be?"

"Sunny, traditionally women don't take sweats with men in the sacred sweat lodge. I respect the Cahuilla tradition and it is unfortunate that you don't have the right parts, but since this is my own personal sweat house, I don't think we'll anger the spirits."

I looked at Daniel, his unbuttoned shirt blowing lightly in the breeze exposing a well-muscled chest. "I'm not sure ..."

He looked into my eyes. There was something different in his manner. "Remember, I learned about my people's history in college." He laughed, "It was years before I spoke with the elders and learned the truth from the stories they told me. I knew I was different. He ..." Daniel paused. "I never wanted to be a medicine man, but ..." He hesitated, "Sunny, when I saw you at the Casino I was overwhelmed by the spirit voices. I *knew* that you were for me." He chuckled and I thought he seemed almost embarrassed, "Do you think you could accept me as an ordinary man?"

"Daniel ..." I stammered.

"Sunny, don't worry." He grinned, "It was Antonio, not I, who followed the old ways of the medicine man." He hesitated, "Antonio took the dark path, remember? I told you, didn't I?" and then he put his arms around me.

I blurted out, "Daniel, are you trying to seduce me?" I had to laugh at myself.

He put his head back and roared with laughter, a rich, rolling laughter. "It has crossed my mind. Does it make you uncomfortable?"

I turned thirty shades of red, "I ..."

Daniel reached over and began unbuttoning my shirt. "Ummm," he breathed deeply, "Sunny, you don't know how long I have wanted to do this."

He slowly undressed me. "You are beautiful like the moon." At first his hands caressed my breasts and then he leaned over and kissed the nipples. "Coyote loved Lady Moon," he whispered hoarsely, "and she fled up into the sky. Stay with me, my lady moon." He slipped off his shirt and unzipped his jeans.

"Daniel ..." I wanted him to stop but I couldn't get the words out. He put his finger over my lips and stroked them. "Shh."

He pulled me down on a blanket and covered me with his body. He explored my body, learning each place, and then he entered me. His lovemaking should have been tender and slow, but it was harsh and demanding. Still, my desire came fiercely alive. Again and again I reached the moment when I couldn't prolong my ecstasy.

Afterward, we retreated into the sweat lodge. "Before you're finished with the sweat, your whole body will feel clean." He laughed quietly as though he knew something I didn't.

He was so right. And later we made love again in his bed. Exhausted, I fell asleep in his arms. It was almost three in the morning when the earthquake struck. I heard the ominous sounds coming from the north and then pictures tumbled off walls and dishes fell from the cupboards. The electricity went off and I was sitting in the dark alone. I was terrified. Would the Colorado River flood into the valley? Was this the *big one?* I screamed, "Daniel?"

He was standing at the foot of the bed. "Sunny, I'm sorry. I meant it as a joke, but things got out of control. I wanted to get even. I never intended to take it so far."

"What are you talking about?"

"Never mind, I think we'd better go outside."

Then the nightmare began. I heard a truck pull up into the driveway. A shadowy figure opened the front door. His flashlight blinded me. "Sunny? Antonio? What the hell are you doing here?"

In horror, I glanced back at the man I thought was Daniel. It was Antonio, I knew him now. He'd played the part of Daniel so well that I hadn't suspected it was Antonio who'd roused long dead sexuality from the depths of my being. Truly he followed the dark path and he'd taken me with him.

Antonio pulled himself up to his full height and laughed triumphantly. "It seems I am more successful as you than you are as yourself."

Daniel's face showed no emotion. "Leave now. You've broken all the bonds of family. I can never forgive you for this abomination."

"Dear brother, I am going. Create harmony of spirit from this." Antonio's eyes blazed with exultation. "You will remember my power all your days." Antonio walked away, smirking and guffawing. He'd won a terrible victory and cared nothing for those who were vanquished. His belated apology to me meant nothing.

Daniel walked hesitantly toward me and held me as I sobbed inconsolably in his arms. "Sunny, I'm so sorry. I ..." We stood there unable to speak, shaken by the enormity of Antonio's betrayal. Finally, Daniel led me into his house. "Sunny, there are no words to change what happened here. I should have known. It was my fault."

"No, Daniel." I sank onto the couch and he sat beside me and put his arms around me until I fell into a restless sleep.

In the evening, I woke to find Daniel cooking a small meal of tortilla sand beans. On the table was an enormous pitcher of orange juice swimming in crushed ice and a nearly empty bottle of Cuervo Gold Tequila.

"I think I need another sweat, Daniel. I feel so dirty."

"I understand. I'll get it ready."

I nodded.

Daniel murmured as if to no one, "You know, I built this myself. I used mesquite limbs and date palm fronds and an old plastic tarp. I got the rocks from a local sand and gravel company, and converted a propane barbecue to heat them. I changed the old songs and prayed for forgiveness. I tried to make myself right with my world. I never expected it would be used ..." He had tears in his eyes, "... that way. Lucy, Mary, Paulo, and now you. It's never enough. Maybe Antonio was right."

He carried the red-hot ricks to the sweathouse in a steel bucket and then filled another one with water. He gave me a metal coffee mug to pour a little water onto the heated bricks.

I had never seen such despair on his face, not even after Mary's murder. "Sunny, go in. I'll wait for you." Daniel didn't come into the sweat lodge with me.

I was still shaken, but the hot steam was therapeutic. I stayed in the sweat lodge until every pore in my body felt cleansed. I wondered what terrible secret Daniel kept hidden inside. I wondered even more whether I'd know that it wasn't Daniel. Somehow I must have known. My body was clean, but my spirit was hemorrhaging.

Daniel had rigged up an outside shower near the sweathouse, cold water only. After the sweat and the shower, he wrapped me in a huge bath towel and we sat on cushions in his screened porch. He brought out two tall glasses of water, no ice, and as we sipped the sweet well water, we talked and talked and talked about everything, anything: God, the universe, stories from his childhood, and from mine; but never a word about what happened between Antonio and me.

I drove home in turmoil. When I walked up to the door of the trailer, Antonio was standing there. "I cannot undo what has been done. My heart bleeds for what happened. All I can do is lend you what strength I have. I can help. Sunny. You must renew your spirit."

I felt my gorge rise. "Damn you!"

It was like Antonio didn't see or hear me. "I caused this pain and for that I am eternally sorry. This was between Daniel and me. I never intended to hurt you. Please believe me."

"How can I?"

He put both of his hands on my shoulders and looked into my eyes. I tried to close my eyes and shake off his hands but I couldn't move. "You must decide. Each spirit knows where to go to find renewal and strength. If you can't trust me, trust yourself and ask for guidance."

"You bastard! Do you think that I'm going to listen to any of your hocus pocus? You might as well have raped me."

"Sunny, I think you knew it was me." Antonio's hands were shaking. "You must have known that Daniel wasn't interested in you as a woman." Suddenly he pulled his hands away as though they were burned by touching me. "I'm not the bad guy. Daniel started all this in motion. He came back from the university crowing with his degrees. I was so proud of him. I took him to a sacred site. The camp was intact. The people had left their ollas, baskets, and smoking pipes. There was even firewood cut and ready to use. I hoped he could tell me what happened.

"I knew our people had gone there for generations and then one day, they left everything behind and they never came back. I burned to know why. But Daniel didn't understand. He brought a colleague from his college and showed him the site. This man had no spirit, only greed. He must have returned later. Everything of value was stolen. He sold the artifacts, destroyed any chance of solving the mystery. I will not tell you how, but I discovered the names of the collectors who bought the artifacts. I raised the money, bought them and returned them to the site. Jerry Branson was one of those who wouldn't return them no matter how much money I offered.

"I used my power to convince him, but somehow it went wrong. I knew nothing of the price the rest of you would pay until it was too late. Jerry had his own demons and I tried to use them for the good of my people."

"You had no right!"

Antonio's face hardened. "Perhaps ... still, I'm offering you my power to help you find your path."

"I want nothing from you! You disgust me!"

"So be it then. But your precious Daniel isn't what you think." Antonio waved his hands as though he were pushing me away. He never touched me, but I fell back, nauseated and dizzy. When my vision cleared, Antonio was gone.

Chapter 58

October 17, 1999
Marietta Ranch

That night I dreamed. In my dream I saw a fiery meteorite falling from the sky. It came to Earth and buried itself into the desert sand. I walked toward where it had fallen. It rose out of the gravel wash, unique in its red color. It was the red brown breast of Mother Earth, inviting me to share her strength. She called to me, "Come, put away all resistance, fear, and anger. Be as you were in the beginning of time. Be one with your spirit. You have been here in my embrace. I will be with you."

I didn't have to be hit on the head. It was time to go, but not to Red Dome. That led to Antonio and disaster. Max and I would ride up the canyon as far as we could go.

It was still dark, but I prepared my hasty pack, put on my jeans, sweatshirt, and an old pair of boots. After I fed Chowder, I made sure I left a bowl of water, some dried kibble, and a lot of newspaper for the pup. She wriggled and begged to be petted. "Poor little no-name pup." She rolled over on her back and I scratched her kicky spot. "I promise you'll have a name when I get back."

I took Max a couple of carrots, put on his blanket, saddle, and bridle. I threw saddle bags on and tied them down, then the sleeping bag. I put the hasty pack on my back and put my foot in the stirrup and threw my leg over the saddle. Max was exuberant, mirroring my own determination to be on the way.

I wasn't surprised to see Daniel; I almost expected it, but my eyesight seemed to be a little blurred. I shook my head to see more clearly. Max sidestepped and surprised me, but I didn't lose my seat.

"No matter what you find, it will be the beginning to a new life. I will be there if you need help on your journey. I have the power. Don't be afraid. Let your thoughts and feelings flow through you.

Allow every thought its time, every feeling its merit. You will find your own place of power."

How many times had I heard him tell me that? Still I entreated, "How can I believe what you say? You couldn't stop Antonio. I still feel so vulnerable."

"That is your strength; to be affected by your experiences is not weakness. Take the risk."

Daniel's image disappeared but I could still feel his presence when Leon tromped out of the horse barn leading Durango. "Sunny, wait up! Daniel said you were going on a ride up Lost Mine Canyon. I thought I'd pack some supplies on ol' Durango here. Food and water for the animals and some cold weather gear for you. Tends to get a bit nippy at night." Leon grinned at me. "Should be enough for a few days anyway."

"Leon, my dear friend, thank you."

Leon's eyes beamed and a huge smile crinkled his weathered cheeks, "I put in a couple of treats for you, too."

Just as the sun peeked over the chocolate mountains, I rode Max and led Durango out the back gate up the wash that would take us to the trailhead of Lost Mine Canyon. Not a cloud in the sky. The only sound was the scrunching of hooves in the gravel wash. Daniel and Leon had both blessed my journey and my heart was as light as an eagle's feather.

www.ingramcontent.com/pod-product-compliance
Lightning Source LLC
Chambersburg PA
CBHW031107260626
47172CB00001B/261